The MURDER
OF MAYOR MALADY

Published by Richardson Publishing Limited.
www.richardsonpublishing.com

10 9 8 7 6 5 4

© 2023 Richardson Publishing Limited.

Puzzles by Dan Moore.

Design and layout by Clarity Media Limited.

Cover design by Hannah Wadham.

ISBN 978-1-913602-38-3

Printed and bound by CPI Group (UK) Ltd, Croydon CR0 4YY.

A catalogue record for this book is available from the British Library.

If you would like to comment on any aspect of this book, please contact us at:
E-mail: littleriddlewood@richardsonpublishing.com

INTRODUCTION

Welcome to Little Riddlewood, a quaint village in which things of great interest do not happen very often. Since its early days, the village has prided itself on its motto *semper eadem* – meaning "always the same", which was also a motto of Queen Elizabeth I. Whilst the world around them changed at a dizzying pace, things were much the same from year to year in this genteel locale. That all changed recently with the sensational murder of the popular stalwart of the local community, Mayor Malady.

This puzzle book details the crime and its aftermath, alongside the exploits of a group of intrepid amateur sleuths in the village (Ben, Gladys, Emily and Harold) who set out to assist the local police in identifying suspects and a motive for the crime, ultimately leading to the identification of the perpetrator.

The pages that follow contain a narrative element accompanying each of the puzzles, and it is therefore designed to be solved in order from beginning to end. Whilst, in almost all cases, no knowledge of previous puzzles is required to solve others, later puzzles may refer back to answers from previous puzzles so can act as spoilers if they are solved out of order.

The book contains a large range of different puzzle types and these will require a range of skills to solve. These include logic, maths, codebreaking, pattern recognition, spatial awareness and lateral thinking. They also purposefully encompass a range of difficulties, so you will find yourself solving some very quickly whilst others will present a stiffer challenge. If you get stuck, try thinking of as many angles as you can to help you proceed with a puzzle before giving up.

Solutions for all puzzles are included at the back of the book, with the aim of providing an explanation as to how each answer is derived where it is useful to do so, and not just the solution itself. There is also a codes section at the back of the book (pages 222-223) that will help you solve some of the puzzles in the book.

There are over 90 puzzling challenges to tackle in this book, all themed around the team of four as they assist Inspector Pointer in his mission to solve the crime and arrest the murderer. Once you've solved all the puzzles, there is a final challenge for you to tackle at the end of page 221.

I hope you enjoy solving the puzzles alongside the intrepid team of Ben, Gladys, Emily and Harold, as they try to restore peace and order to the village of Little Riddlewood by ensuring the identification, and arrest, of the murderer.

Good luck!

CHAPTER 1

MURDER AT THE MANOR

1. SET THE SCENE

MAYOR MALADY has been found murdered in his drawing room at Little Riddlewood Manor. Although not an official title, he was affectionately known as Mayor by the locals due to his political prowess and strong involvement in the running of the community. A group of amateur sleuths consisting of Ben, Emily, Gladys, and Harold have been called as consultants, a day after the murder, to help with the ongoing inquiries. The officer at the crime scene has produced two photographs below taken in the drawing room mere minutes after the mayor's body was discovered at 6pm. The officer is of the belief that the two photographs were taken within seconds of each other, however Gladys pointed out six reasons why this cannot be the case. Can you see why?

BEN   GLADYS   EMILY   HAROLD

Six things have been spotted at the crime scene that suggest that a significant amount of time has passed. A number of items within the room could have been used to commit the fatal crime. Little Riddlewood Manor, being the residence of Mayor Malady, is always full of staff and many people enter and exit the residence each day. Any person who had a meeting with the mayor yesterday would have had ample opportunity. It is the job of this team of sleuths to identify the murder weapon, gather evidence, and work out the motive of the person who could have enacted this awful murder.

2. KILLING TIME

THE GANG ask the officer if the mayor's staff had any comments on the crime scene. They confirm that unfortunately the only person to have entered the room where the murder was committed earlier in the day was his secretary who brought the mayor his post just before his 9am meeting. She confirmed there was no wine glass present in the room at the time but was otherwise unhelpful. The gang then ask the officer if anything was found on Mayor Malady and they are presented with a notebook. Inside there is a cryptic message below which mentions a name 'Silvia'. Ben and Emily decipher the note in record time! Can you find a series of times hidden within the message?

> Baker's Dozen:
> Playing cards in a pack
>
> Planets in the solar system:
> Hours in the day
>
> Vowels: States of America
>
> Silvia

BEN   EMILY

3. NAME THE DAY

SILVIA has appeared to have met with the mayor previously at these times. It's vital that Silvia is added to the list of suspects.

Whilst exploring Mayor Malady's study, the team encounter his calendar with a number of appointments scheduled from the past month. Harold spots a name hidden in the calendar and urges the group to take a closer look. Are you able to identify what Harold has seen with his trained logical eye?

SUN	MON	TUE	WED	THU	FRI	SAT
November							
30	31	1	2 Meeting 3pm	3	4 ✳	5
6	7	8 ✳	9 ✳	10 ✳	11	12 Party 8pm
13 Meeting 11:30am	14	15	16	17 Dentist 10am	18	19
20 ✳	21 ✳	22	23	24 Bridge 7:30pm	25	26
27	28	29 Dinner with Joneses 7pm	30	1	2	3

HAROLD

4. CRIMINAL RECORD

IT APPEARS THAT Mayor Malady met with someone named Judith over the course of the last month.

Next to the mayor's bookcase sits an impressive record collection. Emily and Ben notice something odd with the records that are displayed next to the record player and suspect that they may not be what they seem. Can you see why, and name another suspect in the process?

5. COMPARE NOTES

THE GROUP have discovered yet another person to add to their list of suspects!

Gladys suggests searching through the wastepaper bin in the study of Mayor Malady's manor. She proposes that the murderer might have attempted to throw away any evidence even if poorly executed. Within the rubbish the team spot five pieces of paper folded over. Gladys identifies another name straight away. Can you?

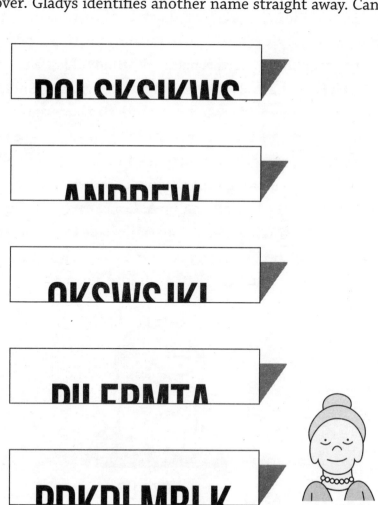

GLADYS

6. WATCH YOUR STEP

WHILST THE REST of the papers are jumbled nonsense, one name stands out from amongst the collection. The team wonder who this mysterious Andrew could be...

Harold, being an ex-policeman, wonders if there were any issues with the protection of the manor and the mayor himself. He consults with the police officer protecting the crime scene for a map showing the designated patrol of each security guard at the manor. It seems like today's map is missing vital details as to the boundaries of the patrol. Without this being mapped, anyone could have strayed from their designated route without being questioned. Mark in the boundaries between each of the regions. Each region is either rectangular or square in shape. A number in the grid indicates the number of squares in each region, and one number per region is shown in the grid. Once you have marked in all the boundaries, sum up the sizes of the regions containing each identical shape in the order circles, squares, triangle, pentagon, cross and star. Can you find a way to convert the six numbers that result into a name?

HAROLD

	2	16						[circle]	
[circle]	2								
3		[square]			6		4		
[star]				6					2
		8					3		[square]
5					12		6		
		[pentagon]							
		2					[square]	3	
2			[cross]					9	
	4					2	3		[triangle]

7. GUNNING FOR SOMEONE

GLADYS discovers from her investigation that a gun has been stashed in the drawing room of the manor. She asks the head security guard to provide images of each of the guns that the security guards handle. She manages to match the image of the gun recovered from the crime scene to one of the images of the guns below in no time at all! Are you also up to the task? The initials displayed on the matching gun will be vital to discovering yet another suspect in this case.

GLADYS

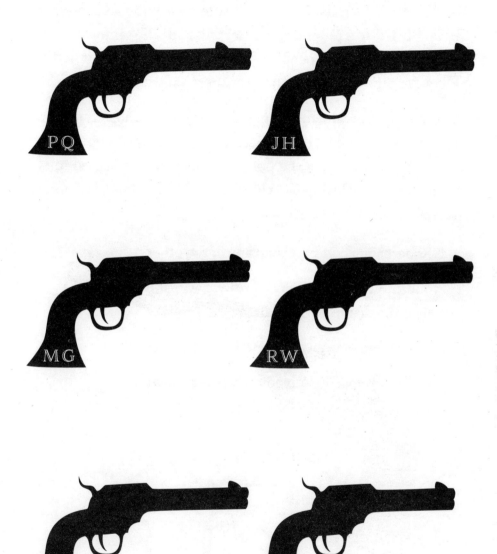

8. SIGN OF THE TIMES

THESE INITIALS must be those of someone who had access, at the very least, to a potential murder weapon. The senior sleuths request a log of all the people who had access to the manor yesterday. Perhaps the people on the suspect list will have signed in.

The group narrow down the list of suspects to those found in the bank below the logbook. Harold's final task is to figure out when each person from the potential suspects list signed in at the manor by analysing the clues provided. Are you also up to the challenge?

1. Robert signed in later than any of the other suspects.

2. Judith signed in earlier than Silvia, whilst Silvia signed in at the manor before Callum.

3. Richie signed in later than Callum and Andrew.

4. Andrew signed in immediately before Callum.

HAROLD

NAME	TIME ENTERED
Bob Cross	9:00am
Amanda Krauss	3:00pm
Agnes McDonald	4:30pm

POTENTIAL SUSPECTS

JUDITH KIRTON   SILVIA TAYLOR   ANDREW GATLIN

CALLUM LOZANO   RICHIE MEDDIT   ROBERT WILSON

2:20pm 10:30am 8:15am 4:10pm 1:40pm 12:35pm

9. TALKING IN CIRCLES

BEN, Emily, Gladys, and Harold meet with each other and the head of the investigation, Inspector Pointer, to share their findings so far. Each possible pairing of the five people will meet with each other once. They only have a limited amount of time to talk to each other, so they have agreed that the discussion between each pairing will last exactly nine minutes. Assuming there is no changeover time between meetings, and the meeting room must be vacated at 5pm, Ben and Harold must work out the latest possible time that the group of five people can start their discussions. Can you do the same in less than two minutes?

HAROLD   BEN   GLADYS   EMILY   INSPECTOR POINTER

SUMMARY

Although the team never expected to encounter such a grisly murder in their sleepy village of Little Riddlewood, they have done exceptionally well to uncover six suspects that all could have committed the crime. As Ben, Emily, Gladys and Harold depart Mayor Malady's manor, they wonder what could possibly lay in store for them.

CHAPTER 2

A MEETING OF MINDS

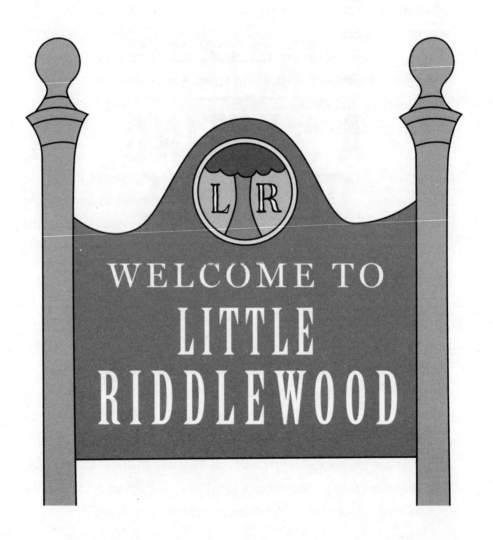

LITTLE RIDDLEWOOD

THE VILLAGE is situated in the heart of the English countryside full of pristine parks, cosy cottages, and inquisitive inhabitants. The residents are set on continuing the impeccable standards of village life that have been established generations prior. However, amongst the luscious foliage and rustic scenery lurks a criminal. It is down to the team of senior sleuths to dig out the weed amongst the (award-winning) roses.

Mayor Malady's murder is the first crime to be reported in Little Riddlewood since the cricket team's county championship trophy was stolen ten years ago. The inhabitants of this idyllic community prize their peace, security, and national village ranking above all else and so are desperate for the culprit to be captured.

Gladys, Harold, Emily, and Ben are on their way to gather more information regarding the six suspects discovered at Little Riddlewood Manor. Where better than the village hall to ask council members, who keep this picturesque town running, a few questions regarding their characters? The hall is known as a bustling community hub where the residents of Little Riddlewood gather to share cake recipes, participate in sporting events, host seasonal fetes, and debate local politics. From all the daily activity that takes place here, someone must have heard or noticed something!

1. IN THE DRIVING SEAT

The first task of our detective ensemble is to correctly plot the route from Little Riddlewood Manor to the village hall. Ben announces the postcode of the hall to the group. The group study a map that they conveniently keep in the glove compartment of Harold's car. Can you correctly plot the route the team need to take to arrive promptly at the village hall and deduce the postcode along the way?

BEN

EMILY

HAROLD

GLADYS

2. SEE THE SIGNS

WHILST STOPPING at a zebra crossing, Emily spots something quite peculiar whilst looking out of the car window. There is something off about the signage pointing to various village landmarks. She asks her companions to look at the signposts and see if they can detect what she has noticed: the name of another location concealed somehow by the signs.

This is a perfect opportunity for the others to brush up their skills of deduction before they arrive at the village hall. Can you help them find the hidden location?

BEN

EMILY

HAROLD

GLADYS

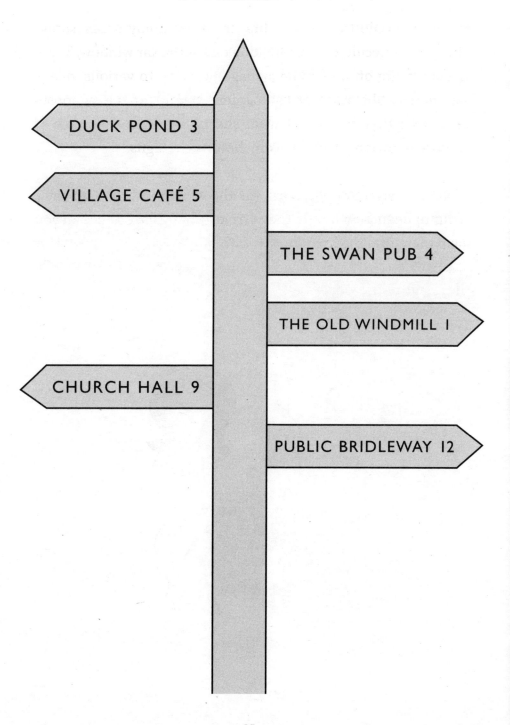

3. HALL OF FAME

AFTER a scenic journey driving past numerous duck ponds, a well-kept bowling green, and many cottages advertising fresh eggs for sale, the sleuthing squad arrive at the most well-known landmark in the village: the village hall. Harold parks the car and the quartet head over to the front of the village hall with a sense of uncertainty as to what may lie ahead.

It is important that the group are aware of any anomalies in their surroundings from this point onwards. Knowing this, Gladys decides to test her aptitude with visual puzzles by taking on the challenge shown here. Which of the silhouettes perfectly match the image of the village hall?

GLADYS

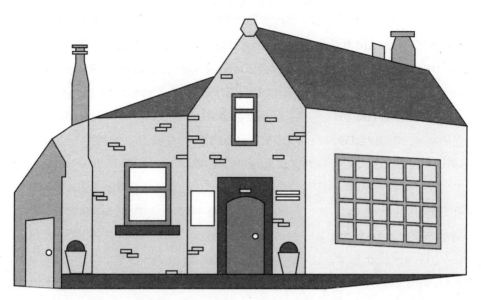

A)   B)

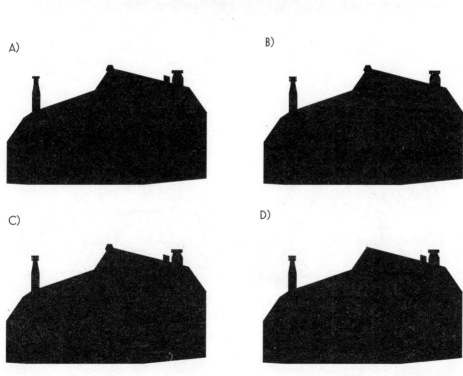

C)   D)

CHAPTER 2   **A MEETING OF MINDS**

4. DUTY CALLS

BEN tries to open the door to the village hall, but it won't budge. Thinking that this is strange for 10am on a Tuesday, he asks the rest of the gang to see if they can spot a key anywhere or, failing that, perhaps a note has been left that they have missed? Emily spies a newly installed intercom system with a note taped alongside it. Written on this note is a numerical code of some sort. Ben's eyes widen with excitement as he grasps the note from her hand. He beckons Harold over to assist him in cracking the message.

Can you crack the code by working out the name of the person they need to ask for when they operate the intercom?

HAROLD   BEN

28

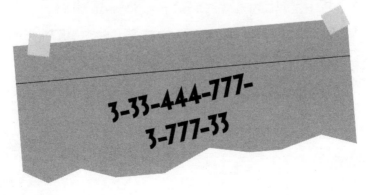

5. THE KEY TO SUCCESS

SUCCESS! A receptionist with a wonderfully cheery tone responds on the intercom and buzzes them in. The lady says she is happy to answer any questions that they may have and introduces herself as Deirdre.

After a discussion around a pot of tea, and far too many shortbread biscuits, the sleuths discover that all their suspects are members of the council and are all very involved with the goings on in the village. Each of them is not shy in raising their grievances, no matter how trivial. Harold, using his skills learnt in the police force, has a good look around and asks if there are files kept on the council members of Little Riddlewood. However, he is told by the receptionist that such files cannot be handed over directly as they may contain sensitive information... but that if someone were to stumble across a key that happened to open the village hall's filing cabinet then that would be out of her control. She then drops a keyring with various keys attached to it on the floor and excuses herself to attend to the essential matter of refilling the teapot.

Gladys seizes the opportunity and pounces on the keys. All she has to do is identify the correct key on the keyring to open the filing cabinet. Which one matches the image provided on the next page?

GLADYS

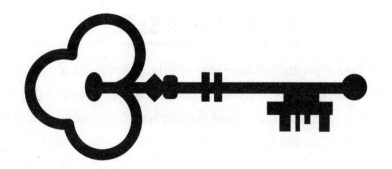

A)

B)

C)

D)

E)

F)

6. CODE NAMES

NOW THAT the filing cabinet is open it is time to analyse the files inside. The only problem is that, presumably due to data protection, all of the names at the top of the files have been encoded. Harold and Ben, assured in their logical and mathematical prowess, are confident that they will be able to figure out who each file is assigned to. Can you reveal the ten names corresponding to the ten files that they look at?

HAROLD   BEN

7. STRANGE SIGNS

PROGRESS has been made now that the sleuths know whose files they are looking at. However, before the group has a chance to look at them a man stumbles in to the village hall looking rather flustered and irritated. He introduces himself as Michael and he works within the council as the planning commissioner. He explains that he has found some mysterious notes all signed with a bizarre signature. Michael is sure that they must have been left late last night as he recalls that there was nothing untoward with his office before he locked up. The culprit must have slid the notes underneath his office door. Michael deduces that it must be someone with an intimate knowledge of the town council both to gain access and ensure they were undetected.

The poor man is obviously very stressed, so the group of sleuths decide to help him by taking a look at one of the notes he has received. They decide that Emily's skills are most suited to this particular conundrum, and indeed soon enough she expresses satisfaction and that she knows who sent the notes. Can you do the same?

EMILY

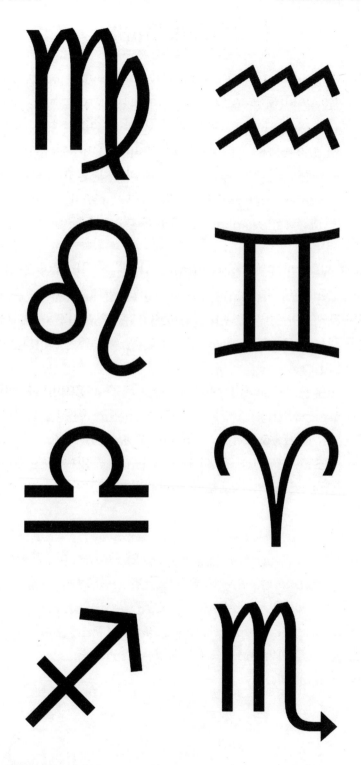

8. ILLUMINATION

MICHAEL tells the group that that is not the first complaint he has received recently. In fact, many letters and emails have been sent to him regarding his work in developing the village of Little Riddlewood. The team look at one another as they simultaneously realise that this could be an interesting avenue along which to proceed with the investigation. How many of their suspects had issues with one or more plans within the village?

Michael ushers them into his office. He has a dedicated folder for complaints and is happy to share what he has been sent. The first complaint is regarding the installation of floodlights at the tennis club which is situated adjacent to a residential road. The complaint relates to the increased levels of light pollution if the plan were to go ahead. Michael shares the plan of the street and the names of the six families with the houses shown below with Harold. Can you work out where each of them live, and hence the name of Michael's prime suspects – the residents of the house closest to the tennis courts?

The Patel family lives two houses further away from the tennis courts than the Smith family, whilst the Rashid family live closer to the courts than the Rogers family. The Smith family and the Richardson family are neighbours, with the Richardson's living closer to the tennis courts. The Rashid and Patel families are neighbours. The Wilson family live closer to the courts than the Richardson family.

HAROLD

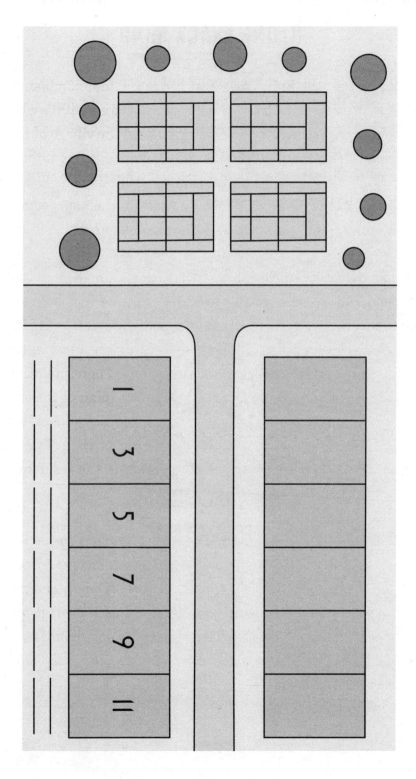

9. ONE TRACK MIND

MICHAEL has also received a complaint regarding the expansion of the train line that passes through the village. Michael passes a coded letter to Harold and explains that it contains a rather scathing review of the proposed plans. Can you work out the contents of this letter and determine just what the the author of the note is so concerned about?

HAROLD

9 1,13 1,16,16,1,12,12,5,4 2,25 20,8,5 16,12,1,14

20,15 5,24,20,5,14,4 20,8,5 18,1,9,12,23,1,25

12,9,14,5. 8,1,22,5 25,15,21 14,15 18,5,7,1,18,4

6,15,18 20,8,5 12,1,14,4 20,8,1,20 20,8,9,19

14,5,23 20,18,1,3,11 23,9,12,12 4,5,19,20,18,15,25,

15,18 20,8,5 23,9,12,4,12,9,6,5 20,8,1,20

12,9,22,5,19 9,14 8,1,18,13,15,14,25 23,9,20,8

21,19 8,5,18,5 9,14 12,9,20,20,12,5

18,9,4,4,12,5,23,15,15,4? 9 23,9,12,12 14,15,20

19,9,13,16,12,25 19,20,1,14,4 2,25 1,14,4 12,5,20

20,8,9,19 8,1,16,16,5,14. 25,15,21 8,1,22,5

2,5,5,14 23,1,18,14,5,4!

10. A GAME OF CHESS

MICHAEL then tells the sleuths that even games can prove controversial in Little Riddlewood! The chess club is currently frustrated with the council as the funding provided to them for their attendance at national competitions has been cut. Not only this, but the fee charged for being allowed to host their club nights in the village hall has almost doubled. All of this was done under the authority of the late mayor.

Michael thinks it is essential that Harold and his companions put themselves in the killer's shoes, and given this dispute it is possible the killer is a keen chess player. Harold takes a look at the logo for the chess club and sees that it contains the puzzle shown here. Harold solves it in short order – can you do likewise?

HAROLD

The letters A, B, C, D and E are a bishop, king, knight, queen and rook in some order. The numbers on two squares of the board indicate how many of the five pieces are attacking those squares. Given this information can you work out the identity of each of the five pieces A-E?

11. VEGETABLE MATTER

YET ANOTHER complaint comes from a member of the organic gardening club. The last organic vegetable growing competition ended in uproar when it was confirmed that a member had used a growth formula on their entry which assisted them in winning the competition. The mayor refused to disqualify the winner because – in his mind at least – it was not clear whether the growth formula used constituted cheating. However, it is safe to say not many people agreed with his decision. Gladys browses the images of the vegetables submitted in the last competition. She must match the larger image of the winning turnip to one of the entries below thus revealing the name of the winner. The remaining contestants must not have been happy with the mayor after his ruling!

GLADYS

ANDREW GATLIN   CHARLES PARKER   MARY WILLIAMS   JOHN GILLESPIE

CALLUM LOZANO   RACHEL VAUGHAN   ANNE ROSS

MARIA LINCOLN   JANE FITZGERALD

12. NAME THE DATE

IT SEEMS THAT both Andrew Gatlin and Callum Lozano could have had a reason to despise the mayor. Neither of them won the vegetable growing competition! It is clear that the village took this competition rather seriously. Is this motive enough to kill?

The receptionist then beckons the group to her office. She explains that a council meeting was held recently where all the main suspects voiced their opinions on the various works planned in the village. They were not positive. She remembers this meeting as being particularly heated which surprised her given they are all council members. Emily asks the receptionist when this meeting took place and she replies, whilst rubbing her temples, that she has a hard time remembering. After some time, she does recall the following information:

The month after the month of the meeting does not contain 31 days; additionally the month in which the meeting took place does not contain the letter R, nor does it contain the letter M. As for the day of the month, it wasn't odd-numbered, nor was it a single-digit date. The digits in the day of the month on which the meeting occurred sum to four.

Can you use this information to work out the date of the meeting?

EMILY

13. MINUTE BY MINUTE

NOW THAT the day and month of the infamous meeting have been established, the group can consult the filing cabinet and bring up the minutes. The receptionist, clearly wanting to assist them, pulls the same trick of leaving the room to fill up the teapot: this is thirsty work after all. When the correct document is found, the team quickly look through the minutes.

The receptionist certainly wasn't lying – some of the comments made in the meeting were scathing! Emily suddenly leaps back in shock: she has noticed a familiar name hidden within the document. The relevant extract from the minutes is shown below, in which the residents discuss the proposed extension to the railway line. Can you spot the name?

"Such a bad idea," exclaimed Judith Kirton, "not in my backyard!"

"In all my years attending these meetings, this is one of the worst", echoed Richie Meddit.

"Let's all calm down", said the chair, as he could sense hackles rising, and saw some
very agitated looking faces glaring at him: clearly this would be a controversial topic.

"If I might be so bold as to offer another opinion", said Andrew Gatlin, "we need to consider that
an extension to the line from Little Riddlewood would make public transport more convenient."

"Thank you for your interjection", said the chairman. "Is anyone else in favour of the proposal?
Are you aware, for instance, that this could bring significant investment to Little Riddlewood?"

"Yes it would", said Robert Wilson. "I'm all in favour of the plan..."

"Let's be honest, you would be", heckled Callum Lozano. "You used to work on the railways!"

"OK, OK, let's not have any personal spats played out in public", urged the chairman anxiously.

"Right, I think that we clearly need to take a vote on this one!"

EMILY

14. ONLY TIME WILL TELL

THE GROUP discuss their findings so far – the visit to the village hall has been more successful than anticipated! The sleuths begin discussing the suspects and as soon as Judith Kirton is mentioned, Michael's ears prick up. Harold asks why he reacted so strongly to the mention of her name.

Michael assures the group that Judith Kirton could not have committed the crime. He states that he met up with Judith at the village hall at 9am on the morning of the murder. At this meeting (which ended up lasting all day) they discussed the upcoming planning works scheduled to take place in the village. During the meeting they discovered they had many mutual interests, and went out for dinner afterwards for a general chat. There was no way, given this, that she could have committed the crime. Ben asks Michael the precise time that they said goodnight to each other. Can you solve this puzzle to reveal the time at which they said goodnight? The answer is the only time that does not appear anywhere in the number grid. Times may be hidden horizontally, vertically or diagonally and in either a forwards or backwards direction.

BEN

8	4	8	4	9	2	0	1	0	4
1	1	9	1	1	2	1	8	5	6
3	5	1	2	5	1	8	8	3	1
1	3	1	1	8	3	1	1	9	2
4	3	9	5	7	0	4	9	0	5
9	2	5	0	0	2	4	1	7	3
6	7	1	2	4	4	5	0	4	7
3	1	0	2	7	2	6	9	5	7
8	1	7	3	2	7	8	1	7	4
2	0	4	5	8	2	2	3	1	4

07:45	14:45	19:18
09:35	15:15	20:31
10:27	15:20	20:45
11:34	16:40	21:05
12:12	17:23	23:14

15. SUSPECT PUZZLE

BEN discreetly checked with the receptionist that Michael was indeed in an all-day meeting with Judith on the day of the murder, and she duly confirmed the meeting took place. The group are therefore satisfied that Judith can be ruled out.

Now that a suspect has been eliminated, the team take a final look at some of the documents in the filing cabinet, and find the puzzle below lurking within. It is the job of Harold to utilise his logical skills and correctly assign each suspect to their age, job, and hobby by using the clues provided. The future of this investigation rests on this task being completed successfully. No pressure, Harold! Can you successfully solve it?

One council member has published over a dozen books about the wildlife found in the sprawling English countryside. In their free time, this author is a budding artist who likes to paint the specimens found in their research. Some of their paintings can be purchased in the village tearoom for a very reasonable price!

The council member in their 40s produces much of the villages fresh milk, eggs, and meat in their job as a farmer. Although they are slightly pricier than supermarket produce, the quality is second to none. Silvia is a regular patient at the local GP practice as she often has real (or imagined) ailments that need attending to. She knows every employee on a first name basis!

Andrew's age is a multiple of five. The 28-year-old is a popular teacher at the local secondary school. As a science teacher, they have been known to teach very exciting lessons and conduct a variety of experiments. They believe hands-on learning is key to a child's development.

The council member who is a doctor also has a keen interest in plants. They love learning about the different structures and properties of rare and common plants. In their free time they can be found in their greenhouse studying their precious plants. Similarly, the eldest council member loves the visual art of flower arranging. This has been their hobby for some 10 years and are an expert in identifying a large range of flowers.

Richie and Silvia have no interest in beekeeping: Silvia is far too afraid that any interaction with a bee may result in an allergic reaction! The teacher is not a fan of hiking. The second-eldest council member has not attended medical school and so would not be able to identify any kind of sting if Silvia were to come to them for help. Robert has been the trusted go-to handyman in the village of Little Riddlewood for a considerable time: as lots of the village buildings are old, he has been inside the homes of many residents to make repairs over the years.

Use the clues above and the cross-referencing table below to help you solve the puzzle and thus fill in the table on the next page.

	28	33	45	59	62	Author	Doctor	Farmer	Handyman	Teacher	Art	Beekeeping	Flower Arranging	Hiking	Horticulture
Andrew															
Callum															
Richie															
Robert															
Silvia															
Art															
Beekeeping															
Flower Arranging															
Hiking															
Horticulture															
Author															
Doctor															
Farmer															
Handyman															
Teacher															

HAROLD

Name	Age	Job	Hobby
Andrew			
Callum			
Richie			
Robert			
Silvia			

SUMMARY

THE TEAM now have a better grasp of the lives of each of the suspects. This information will surely be invaluable to the investigation ahead. Onwards and upwards!

Thanking the receptionist and Michael for their help, Ben, Emily, Gladys, and Harold head back to the car and discuss their findings so far. The village hall proved to be a vital resource for understanding more about the suspects and even helped eliminate one person as the killer. The gang ponder the best course of action as Ben starts the engine. On to the next location!

CHAPTER 3
CLUED IN

1. COPS AND ROBBERS

THE GANG decide that the best course of action is to meet Inspector Pointer at the police station to discuss the evidence gathered from the crime scene. Once they arrive, they are guided to the interview room. It seems that Inspector Pointer arrived some time before the group and has some important police work to attend to first. The sleuths wait patiently for the esteemed detective to return.

Inspector Pointer enters the interview room hurriedly and quickly greets Ben, Emily, Harold and Gladys. In his hand is a file with many pieces of paper stuffed inside. He sits at the desk and sighs with exasperation. It seems that the Inspector has been attempting to solve a robbery in the nearby town of Befuddle-borough. The victim of the robbery has had various precious belongings stolen and the inspector needs to tag each item that has subsequently been recovered during his investigation.

Inspector Pointer apologises for being distracted but he is ada-mant he cannot discuss Mayor Malady's murder investigation until each item has been correctly labelled. Ben and Gladys volunteer to help out with the labelling of items. Can you work out the number that they assigned to each of the following items that were recovered from the robbery: a vase, a ring, a watch and a wallet? Each item is tagged with a different number from 1-10, and numbers around the edge of the grid indicate the sum total of the objects in the respective row or column.

BEN   GLADYS

24

16

37

28

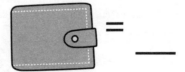

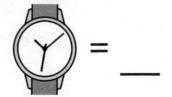

2. BODY LANGUAGE

THE INSPECTOR breathes a sigh of relief. Now the team can focus all their attention on the matter at hand: the developments in the murder of Mayor Malady. Emily explains that through their investigation at the village hall, they have managed to eliminate one suspect out of the six that they had discovered at Little Riddlewood Manor. Harold explains that Judith Kirton should no longer be considered a suspect.

As they explain how they arrived at that conclusion the Inspector nods in approval. He opens the file he has before him and explains that he received a report from the lab which is said to confirm how Mayor Malady died and the method used by the murderer. The first page reveals which part of the body was fatally injured. Emily studies the page and within a few minutes identifies the body part that was affected. Can you do the same by solving the puzzle and creating an anagram of the relevant letters?

EMILY

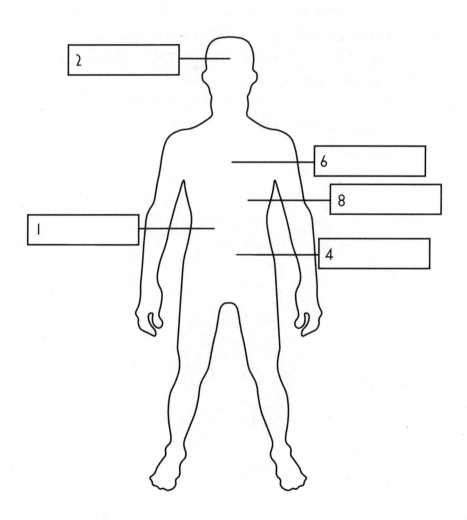

Anagrams
- EAT CHIP
- CRAB REEL
- ACID ARC
- MANLY POUR
- RIG CAST

2

6

8

1

4

3. CAUSE OF DEATH

NOW THAT the gang know which part of the body was fatally affected, they have to deduce what exactly caused the damage. Inspector Pointer pulls another file out of the folder he has on the table and explains that the lab has sent a document that supposedly holds the answer. Unfortunately, the document has been faxed incorrectly and all that they have are two rows of unintelligible symbols. Gladys takes a look at the paper and begins writing something down, before triumphantly revealing that she knows what caused the Mayor's death. Can you work out what she wrote down?

GLADYS

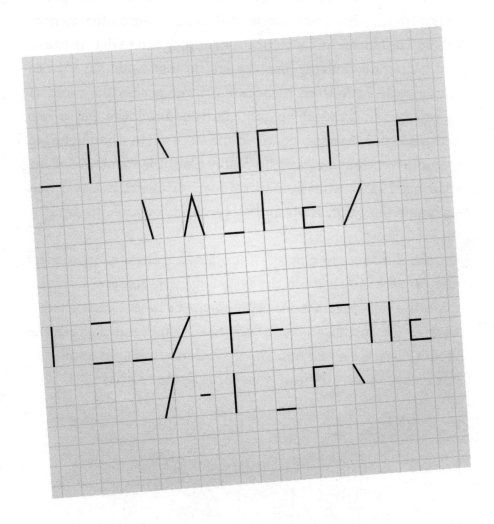

4. PICTURE THIS

THE GROUP discuss how Mayor Malady could have been exposed to the toxic plant. The noise in the room grows louder as Ben, Emily, Harold and Gladys start swapping extensive theories and jotting down every logical scenario that could have led to his death. A little later, Inspector Pointer hushes the room as he explains that the lab has just confirmed that the mayor was poisoned, and has even identified the method the murderer used to get the mayor to ingest the deadly plant. Ben and Gladys are challenged to solve this puzzle in order to discover the answer and within minutes they confirm their result. Can you do the same?

Numbers around the edge of the grid indicate how many consecutive squares to shade in the respective row/column. Commas indicate a gap of at least one blank square between sets of shaded squares. For instance a clue of 4,3 means that somewhere in the region there is a set of four shaded squares, followed by at least one empty square, then another three shaded squares.

BEN   GLADYS

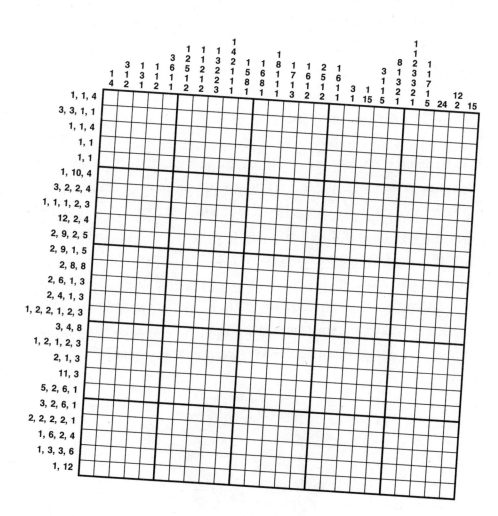

5. A HIDDEN MESSAGE

INSPECTOR POINTER explains to the amateur sleuths that the lab confirmed a small dose of the poison was placed in the Mayor's wine and that it would have taken a while to kill him. Therefore it is hard to pinpoint the exact time he had been poisoned during the course of the day. He urges the team to keep in touch with him and let him know if they make any further progress cracking the case.

As Inspector Pointer exits the room, the gang start to discuss what next steps they should take to continue with their investigation. After a few minutes, Emily suggests that it might be wise to learn more about the plant from which the poison was derived, and the conditions in which it is grown. Perhaps, she posits, that could lead them to the culprit. She suggests visiting her favourite building in all of Little Riddlewood. This location can be revealed by successfully solving the wordsearch puzzle below: can you work out how, and what that location is?

EMILY

```
T  W  A  I  N  E  I  K  L  O  T
E  E  L  G  N  I  M  E  L  F  O
G  Y  A  T  W  O  O  D  O  L  I
I  R  E  T  T  O  P  I  R  L  L
G  N  I  L  W  O  R  C  R  L  E
Y  O  T  S  L  O  T  K  A  E  B
F  T  S  G  H  E  B  E  C  W  R
L  Y  I  N  A  A  H  N  R  R  O
O  L  R  I  D  A  M  S  R  O  W
O  B  H  K  Y  A  U  S  T  E  N
W  E  C  Y  O  J  L  E  W  I  S
```

ATWOOD	ELIOT	POTTER
AUSTEN	FLEMING	ROWLING
BLYTON	GRISHAM	SHELLEY
BROWN	JOYCE	TOLKIEN
CARROLL	KING	TOLSTOY
CHRISTIE	LEE	TWAIN
DAHL	LEWIS	WOOLF
DICKENS	ORWELL	

6. BOOKWORM

THE GROUP bundle into Harold's car, and wonder who would know enough about the plant in question to use it in the murder of the mayor. It is well known that as the village of Little Riddlewood is situated in the heart of the English countryside it is in a data blackspot and therefore it is almost impossible for residents to connect to the internet. The inhabitants of the village are therefore well accustomed to using more traditional means of obtaining information, namely using reference books and encyclopaedias. The culprit must have had to visit the library in order to learn how to grow the plant in question and to extract the compound to formulate the poison.

Emily presents the group (minus Harold who is driving) with a puzzle themed around book genres in order to prepare them for the day ahead. Can you track a continuous path through the grid from beginning to end visiting each square exactly once?

EMILY

O	G	Y	R	E	T	S	Y	M	R
T	C	L	C	A	I	O	R	R	O
H	E	A	I	C	T	N	O	H	H
I	C	S	S	R	E	N	O	Y	T
C	N	A	Y	D	L	L	I	M	Y
W	E	M	S	T	R	I	R	E	D
T	S	O	P	O	H	T	S	M	O
E	Y	R	I	A	I	C	P	E	C
R	S	A	T	N	P	E	Y	R	U
N	F	A	N	A	D	V	E	N	T

Action, Adventure, Classic, Comedy, Dystopian, Epic, Fantasy, Gothic, Horror, Mystery, Myth, Noir, Romance, Spy, Thriller, Western

7. NAME TAG

HAROLD parks the car as the rest of the group head inside Little Riddlewood's library. Inside they are met with the familiar scent of old books. The shelves are stacked full of books, documents and other archival material. There are chairs and sofas dotted around the room with ambient lighting illuminating cosy corners. The smell of mint lingers in the air as the librarian lifts a cup of hot peppermint tea to his lips. The group approach the front desk.

Harold catches up to the group as Ben begins his enquiries. He hopes that the librarian may have noticed someone come in more frequently than usual, or perhaps someone who has been checking out rarely accessed books. He is just about to address the librarian when he notices that the person's name tag does not actually display a name but instead a couple of images: perhaps the librarian is a fellow puzzle fan! Gladys notices Ben's confusion and offers her assistance. Are you able to decipher the name of the librarian by studying the name tag?

GLADYS

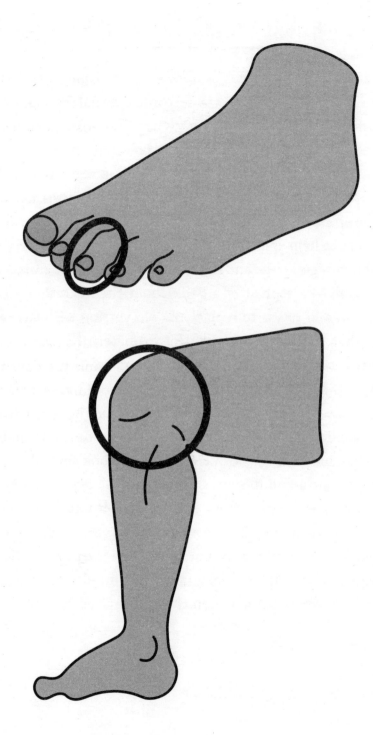

8. BALANCING THE BOOKS

BEN mentions the name tag, and the librarian smiles and says he finds it a good icebreaker, and confirms that he is indeed something of a puzzle fan. Tony then indicates that he is unfortunately too preoccupied with a pressing matter to offer any assistance at the moment, but is willing to help once he has resolved the task in front of him. Harold suggests to the gang that it may be in their best interests to solve the problem themselves to help speed the investigation along. He asks what the problem seems to be and the librarian explains the situation: he has received a reprint of a book about the history of Little Riddlewood and needs to replace the old version with the new version that has been sent in. Unfortunately, he has mixed up the two books and can't tell which version to place on the shelves as they are so similar. Tony gestures to the two books sat neatly on his desk and sighs in frustration: he knows that various spelling mistakes were corrected in the new version but despite looking through both copies of the book several times, he cannot spot any differences. Emily and Gladys take a book each and swap each copy after a few minutes. It takes them next to no time to identify spelling corrections on various pages. Can you circle the lone difference that appears on the page shown as it appears in both the original and the reprinted version of the book, and therefore work out which is the revised version?

The annual horticultural display is the must-see event in Little Riddlewood. For many years generations of amateur and expert gardeners, botanists and florists have battled it out in front of audiences and judges to be crowned by the mayor as the winner of Little Riddlewood's prestigious green fingers award. Expect to encounter perfectly manicured lawns, pristinely organised bouquets and absurdly large marrows expertly grown and maintained by local inhabitants. Make a quick hop across the village green and you will be met with an incredible spread of scones, cakes and sandwiches that can be purchased at the village hall. A perfect way to end the day!

Historically, the Meddits and the Wilsons have triumphed at the display, yet newcomers such as the Gatlins, the Lozanos and the Taylors have quickly challenged the domination of the principal winners. In fact, the rivalry between some of the families has been documented through the generations. On numerous occasions local authorities have had to step in to mediate any disputes that have arisen. One thing is abundantly clear: no matter if you are visiting Little Riddlewood's annual horticultural display to admire the plants or just for the excitement of the competition, you are sure to get more than your money's worth!

54

EMILY

GLADYS

The annual horticultural display is the must-see event in Little Riddlewood. For many years generations of amateur and expert gardeners, botanists and florists have battled it out in front of audiences and judges to be crowned by the mayor as the winner of Little Riddlewood's prestigious green fingers award. Expect to encounter perfectly manicured lawns, pristinely organised bouquets and absurdly large marrows expertly grown and maintained by local inhabitants. Make a quick hop across the village green and you will be met with an incredible spread of scones, cakes and sandwiches that can be purchased at the village hall. A perfect way to end the day!

Historically, the Meddits and the Wilsons have triumphed at the display, yet newcomers such as the Gatlins, the Lozanos and the Taylors have quickly challenged the domination of the principle winners. In fact, the rivalry between some of the families has been documented through the generations. On numerous occasions local authorities have had to step in to mediate any disputes that have arisen. One thing is abundantly clear: no matter if you are visiting Little Riddlewood's annual horticultural display to admire the plants or just for the excitement of the competition, you are sure to get more than your money's worth!

54

9. WRONG NUMBER

THE LIBRARIAN thanks the group profusely for helping him resolve the puzzle so quickly and identifying which is the correct book to place on the shelf. The amateur sleuths then go on to explain how they are searching for information about a particular plant in connection with the unfortunate death of Mayor Malady. The librarian says that it would be very difficult to try and work out who the murderer might be purely by looking at the list of books taken out by each resident over the last few weeks. Nevertheless, he looks at books recently loaned out and notices that some books have been taken out far more frequently than others, and some of them have yet to be returned to the shelves. The librarian has even noted down the ISBN numbers of the books which he planned to create waiting lists for. All the gang has to do is to identify the books strewn around the librarian's desk and place them on the empty trolley next to the reception desk. Ben scans down the list of numbers and smiles to himself. It seems this should not be a hard task for him! Can you circle the correct ISBN numbers that match the numbers on the librarian's note?

BEN

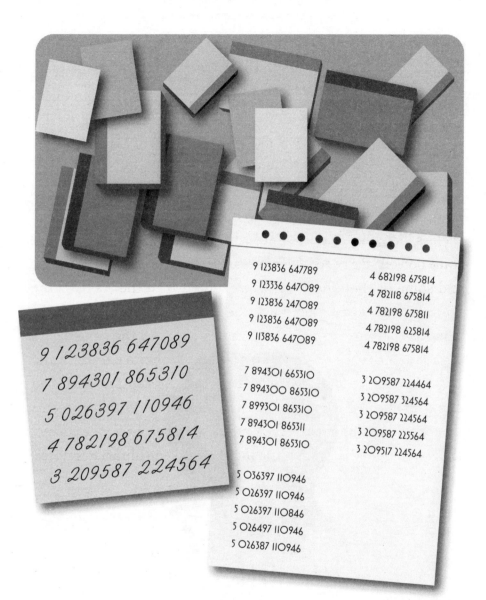

9 123836 647789
9 123336 647089
9 123836 247089
9 123836 647089
9 113836 647089

4 682198 675814
4 782118 675814
4 782198 675811
4 782198 625814
4 782198 675814

7 894301 665310
7 894300 865310
7 899301 865310
7 894301 865311
7 894301 865310

3 209587 224464
3 209587 324564
3 209587 224564
3 209587 225564
3 209517 224564

5 036397 110946
5 026397 110946
5 026397 110846
5 026497 110946
5 026387 110946

9 123836 647089
7 894301 865310
5 026397 110946
4 782198 675814
3 209587 224564

10. CROSS SECTION

NOW THAT the correct books have been identified, the librarian asks the gang to take them to the correct section of the library. Seeing that the gang loved solving puzzles, the librarian quickly created the following brainteaser for them which Emily solved with aplomb. Can you work out what that section is, by solving the puzzle? You must create a word from the letters on each wordwheel opposite, and the word you make must use every letter apart from one on each of the wheels. The words you create are linked somehow. Your leftover letters will then spell out the section of the library to which the books should be returned.

EMILY

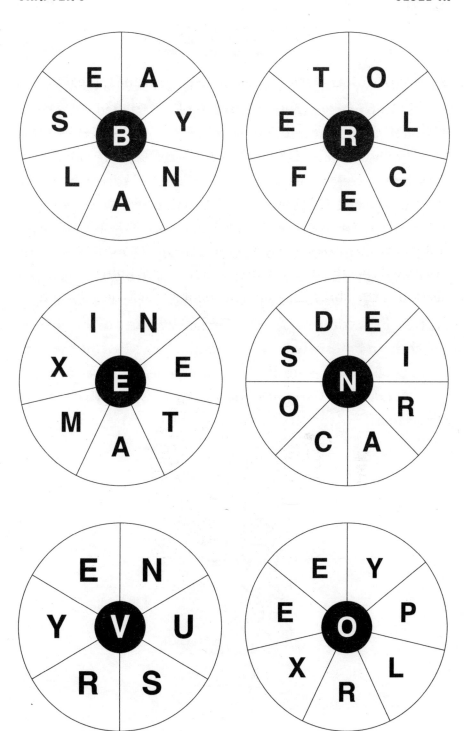

11. TALL TALES

THE TEAM arrive at the correct section of the library. Surely the killer must have come here to look for information to assist them in committing their murderous crime. This is the perfect place to learn about a new plant and to discreetly hatch a plan. Gladys browses the collections of books arranged on the shelves. She can't quite place what is wrong with the current layout, but she senses that these books are all in the wrong position. Harold skims the titles and arrives at the same conclusion. There is something distinctly off with one shelf in particular. Suddenly, Harold is fast at work taking books off the shelf and then placing them back on the shelf. After some minutes he extracts one book from the shelf and presents it to the group. He is adamant that this is the book they need to study in order to learn more about the plant in question. Can you work out how Harold arrived at that conclusion?

HAROLD

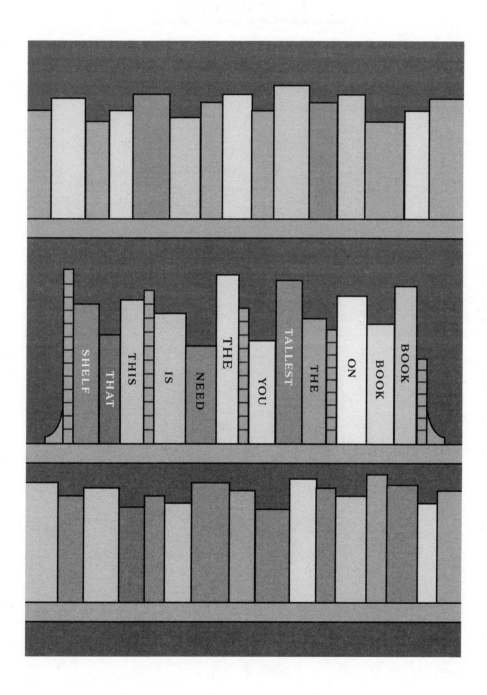

12. A CRACKING CODE

THE TEAM take the book over to a nearby desk to read. They place the book down and turn on the overhead lamp. As they start flicking through the pages, they come across a chapter dedicated to lily of the valley. It appears that a particular passage is written in code. This seems like far more than just a coincidence, so Emily gets straight to work by pulling a notebook from her pocket and tries her best to crack the code. The rest of the gang take a step back and leave her to it. Just as they settle down in an old leather sofa, she returns with the code cracked. Can you work out what the passage reveals?

EMILY

fgnb hvcfibh sise cp ugn yzssne mszbuw iu iw ilmcvuzbu uc nbwkvn ugne zvn mcwiuicbnd ib z wgzde wmcu zbd ugzu ugn wkvvckbdibh wcis iw jnmu lciwu.

Crack the code and write the words below:

13. SHOPPING LIST

EMILY is excited to reveal that she has found a shopping list within the book that has been used as a bookmark. Ben and Gladys are not so thrilled by the discovery as they think that this has nothing to do with the investigation. How can a list of someone's shopping habits help them with a murder inquiry? Harold believes that maybe there could be something here hidden in plain view. After all, he says, it is the duty of the team to pursue every avenue that presents itself. Harold analyses the list with Emily and, just as they thought, a new location is revealed. The group wonder why this information was concealed. There must be something there that the killer doesn't want them to discover. Can you identify the place the gang should visit next?

EMILY   HAROLD

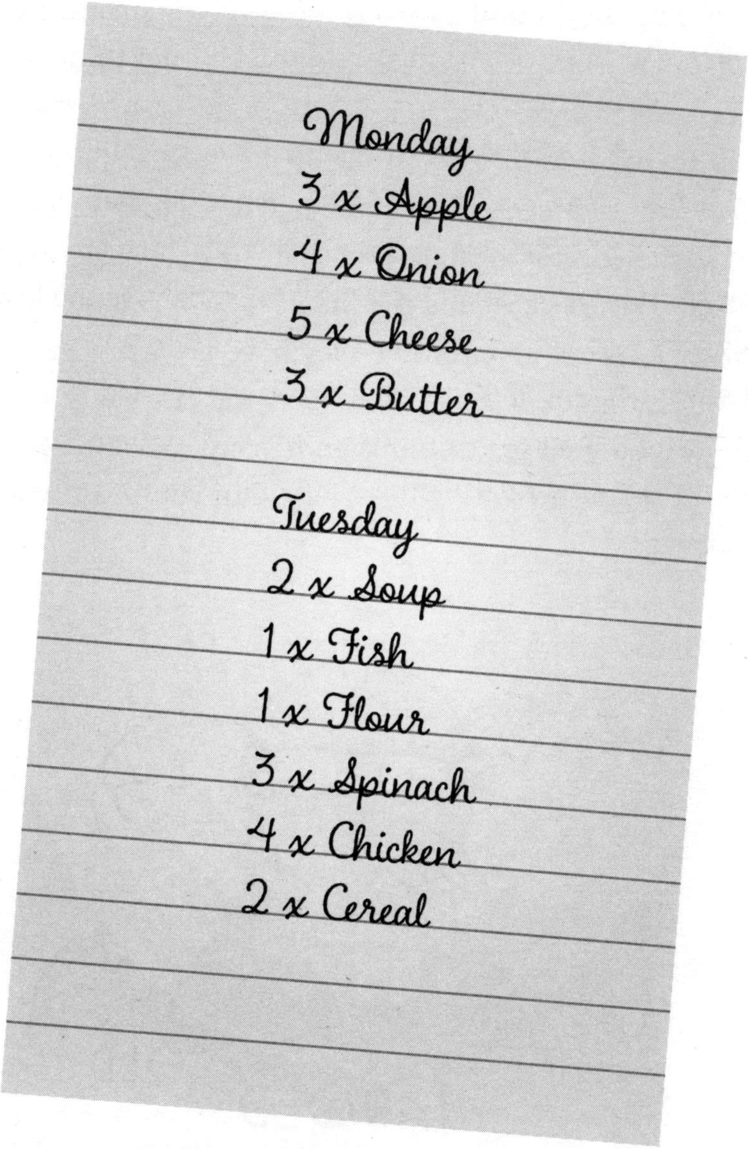

Monday
3 x Apple
4 x Onion
5 x Cheese
3 x Butter

Tuesday
2 x Soup
1 x Fish
1 x Flour
3 x Spinach
4 x Chicken
2 x Cereal

14. EVERY NAME IN THE BOOK

THE LITTLE RIDDLEWOOD library is very open about who borrows the books and so the front of each book lists not just the date on which the book was taken out but also the name of the resident who took out the book on each occasion. The group therefore flip to the front of the book in order to look at the list. However, they notice that instead of words, it contains a series of symbols and that the dates have also been omitted. Harold questions the librarian who states that books now use a recent system that they have brought in that does not use orthodox letters. After studying the sheet for some time Harold manages to translate its contents and his efforts have led to an interesting discovery. Can you identify each of the names?

HAROLD

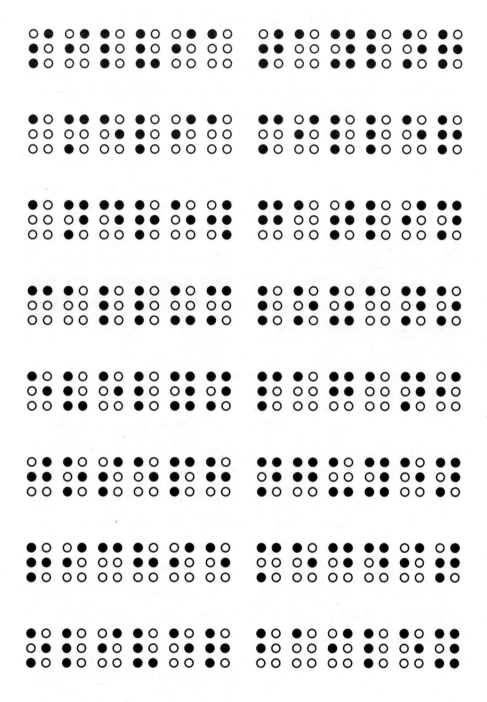

15. IN BLACK AND WHITE

ALL THE SUSPECTS had borrowed the book from the library apart from one, who can therefore almost certainly be eliminated from the investigation. Just to be sure, the team question the librarian about the individual not listed as having taken out the book, and the librarian confirms that this person does not even have a library card so could not have simply spent several hours in the library researching the information they needed. Going by Tony's book on the history of Little Riddlewood, and the fact that Robert Wilson does not own a library card, it is clear that he must not share the same passion for horticulture as his ancestors! Therefore the gang feel confident in eliminating him from the investigation.

Before leaving the library and moving on, the group ask the librarian for the address of the local post office alongside the name of the branch manager so that they can ask them a few questions. The librarian receives a phone call just as he is about to answer, but having seen how much the group enjoy solving puzzles, he manages to scribble a code on a sticky note for them whilst he is on the phone that simply says "Branch manager's name is..." followed by a series of strange symbols. Gladys passes the note to Emily and Harold who have the best chance of solving this particular conundrum. Her assumption is correct as they solve the puzzle in record time and make their way back to the car. Can you do the same?

HAROLD　　　　　EMILY

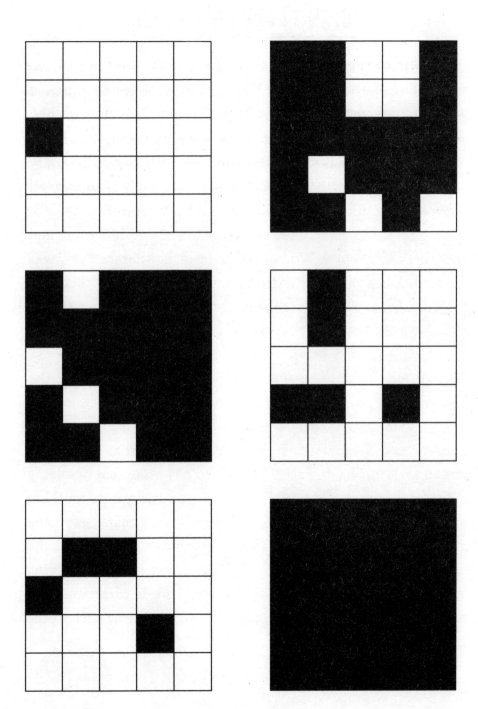

SUMMARY

ALTHOUGH the group had only expected to learn more about the plant that fatally killed Mayor Malady, they also managed to eliminate another suspect from their investigation. As Ben, Emily, Gladys and Harold once again travel through the scenic village of Little Riddlewood, each ponder what could possibly be uncovered at their next location: the post office. Onwards and upwards!

CHAPTER 4

MANNING THE POST

1. DOOR TO DOOR

THE SCENIC journey through Little Riddlewood never gets old for these amateur sleuths. With the sun shining brightly, the team take a moment to enjoy the sound of the birds singing and flitting between the lush trees as they travel through the winding roads. Before long the team turn in to the post office car park.

Before entering the post office, Emily challenges Ben to complete a maths puzzle. She noticed he had rather little to do in the library and, expecting that he might find a warm-up helpful, she opens her notebook and begins to sketch out a series of front doors. Ben spots that most of the doors have door numbers and letterboxes and also notes that some of the doors do not have door numbers on them. Emily explains that numbers that are present on the doors follow a very particular pattern. She asks Ben to fill in the missing numbers in – can you do the same?

BEN

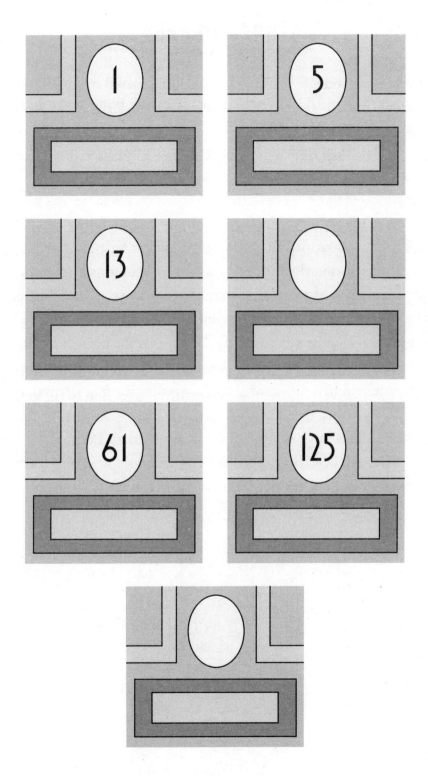

2. STAMP OF APPROVAL

ENTERING the post office, the group spy a postal worker tending to customer queries, weighing parcels and filing away letters which will later be distributed to the residents of Little Riddlewood. The team wait in the queue politely for their turn at the front desk. Once it is their turn to approach, they realise that the worker is none other than the branch manager herself whom the team identify by reading her name badge. Emily begins to explain the situation but she hardly manages to speak two words when she is quietly hushed. Audrey is studiously examining five envelopes. She explains that another worker has identified that one of the five envelopes should not be distributed to its intended recipient due to an invalid stamp. The branch manager has been studying the envelopes in-between serving customers and cannot find a difference. Knowing that the branch manager is unlikely to aid them in their investigation until this problem is resolved, Gladys volunteers her assistance. Because of her keen artistic eye, she identifies the fraudulent stamp almost immediately. Can you also identify the forgery?

GLADYS

3. MISSING CONNECTIONS

NOW THAT THE FORGERY has been identified, the group hope to question the branch manager about the mysterious shopping list found during their visit to the library. The branch manager ensures that all the customers within the post office have been served before shutting the branch temporarily. This building, she explains, is the beating heart of the village and every resident of Little Riddlewood frequents the post office to collect their parcels and other correspondence. Harold asks if it is possible for him and the team to take a look around the premises. He explains how the person who killed Mayor Malady must have collected something from the post office that was integral to their planning as they disguised this location within a coded shopping list. They mention the list of suspects to the branch manager, who recalls that the suspects listed only collected one parcel each in the past month.

The branch manager is keen to help the team, however laments the fact that the conveyor belt to the sorting machine has malfunctioned. Until an engineer attends the premises, all staff have been ordered to keep away from the equipment and any of the back rooms of the post office. Harold promptly rolls up his sleeves and marches over to the control panel to the sorting machine. After a brief analysis of the situation, he concludes that the panel itself needs to be rewired. All he needs to do is connect the correct amount of wires to the numbered points on the circuit board. In no time at all the team hears a steady hum of the machinery as it begins switching on. Harold must have been successful in his task! Can you similarly place the correct wires between the numbered points in the sorting machine circuit board?

Connect every piece of the sorting machine (represented by circles) into a single interconnected group. To do this draw wires between pieces of the machine. The number in each circle states how many wires must be connected to that piece of the machine. Wires cannot cross each other, can only be drawn horizontally or vertically, and there can be a maximum of two wires between any pair of pieces of the sorting machine.

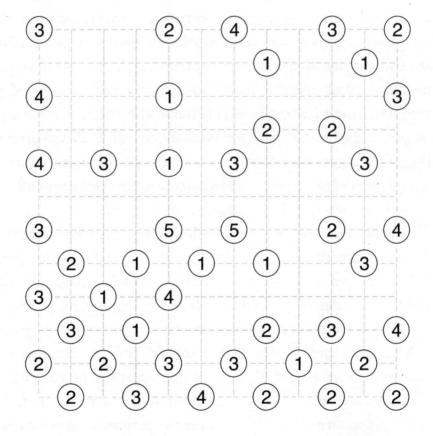

HAROLD

4. HANDLE IT

THE TEAM ask if it is now safe for them to investigate the area around the sorting machine. Unfortunately, Audrey explains, there is still one more task to complete. She bends down underneath the front desk and rummages around the shelves. In a few moments she returns with a box in her arms and asks the team to examine the contents. Inside are various different hand cranks with a strangely shaped handle attached to each. She gestures towards the machinery and the sleuths spy a series of other cranks with these handles attached. The team assess that each hand crank (with handle) is attached to one gear. They note that there is one gear without a handle or hand crank attached. The branch manager asks Harold and Gladys to insert the correct crank from the box into the machinery. She assures them that the sorting machine follows a specific logic so only one of the handles will fit this particular configuration. After a short discussion, the pair manage to choose the correct hand crank. Are you able to do the same?

HAROLD

GLADYS

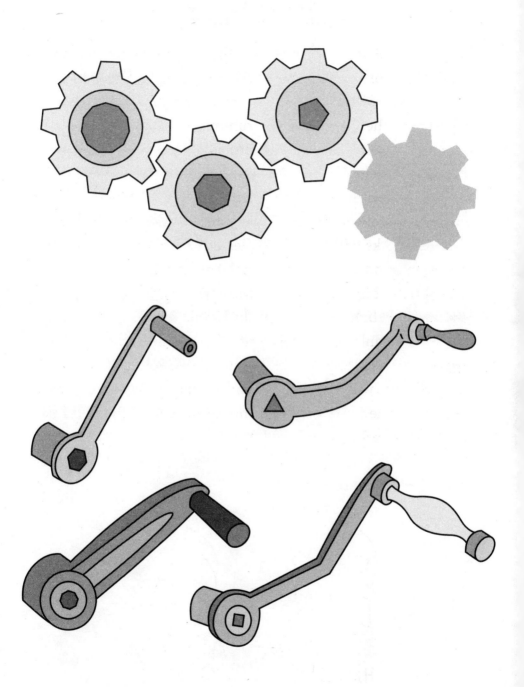

5. KEPT IN THE LOOP

NOW THE SORTING machine is working, Harold poses the group a new challenge. Through his work in repairing the machine, he has had a chance to track the route of the conveyor belt. He wonders if the group, with limited information, can identify the route of one of the main conveyor belts as it makes its way through the post office. He presents Ben, Emily and Gladys with the basic blueprints of the sorting machine. With a quick look at the plans the rest of the group dive into the task. Can you match the group's capabilities and identify the route of the conveyor belt?

Draw a single loop in the grid that visits all squares that are neither clue squares, nor shaded black. Clue squares (containing numbers and arrows) indicate how many squares in the direction of the arrow are to be shaded black and are not part of the loop. Shaded squares cannot touch each other horizontally or vertically. Shaded squares may not all be clued. The loop moves horizontally or vertically through squares and may turn 90 degrees inside a square.

GLADYS   BEN   EMILY

6. SWAPPING NOTES

WITH THE SORTING MACHINE now working, Audrey feels confident in helping the investigative team with their enquiries. The branch manager first helps the group by presenting them with a file full of scraps of paper. Emily is confused as she browses the contents. It is apparent that the slips of paper inside are portions of documents. They have either been ripped or cut and they are all jumbled inside the folder. The branch manager explains that the slips of paper are notices which are sent out to the public once a package they have ordered has arrived at the post office branch. In order to collect their delivery, the customer MUST hand over each notice to a member of staff. Once they are handed back to the postal worker, the notices are ripped into pieces and filed away for the next month before being permanently destroyed. This is to protect customer information whilst also keeping proof that the parcel has been collected. The branch manager confirms that each one of the suspects collected a parcel within the last month and so the parcel information should be present within the file. It is down to the team to piece together the notices to uncover any useful information regarding each of the parcels. Gladys steps up to take the lead and begins frantically shuffling the pieces together. Only a few minutes pass before the notices are restored. Can you identify the collection number of each parcel as well as the time and date that each suspect collected their item?

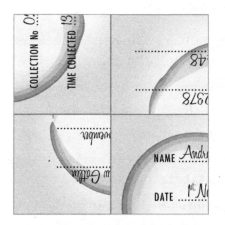

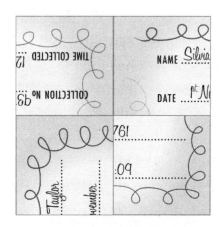

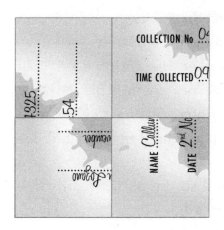

GLADYS

7. THINK OUTSIDE THE BOX

GLADYS has now uncovered the number of the parcel collected by each suspect. The branch manager informs the group that the parcels that each suspect collected were stamped on each side with a symbol. The branch manager turns over the pages on a clipboard and hands Gladys the path that each package took. Whilst tapping on the page, the branch manager explains that the symbol that was at the TOP of the box after its journey through the various conveyor belts in the sorting office confirms which section each parcel is being held in. The team turn to Gladys as they recognise that she is most suited for this job. After making various gestures with her hands and scribbling some notes, Gladys is able to identify which parcels are held in which section of the sorting office. Use the cube net below to fill in the correct symbol in each empty square in each path on the next page. The symbol at the end of each path will give the location of each parcel.

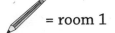 = room 1

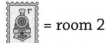 = room 2

 = room 3

 = room 4

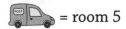 = room 5

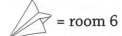 = room 6

Path 1
Collection Number: 02378

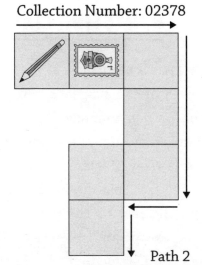

Path 2
Collection Number: 93761

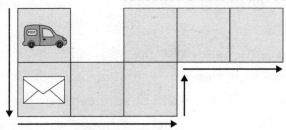

Path 3
Collection Number: 04325

Path 4
Collection Number: 85309

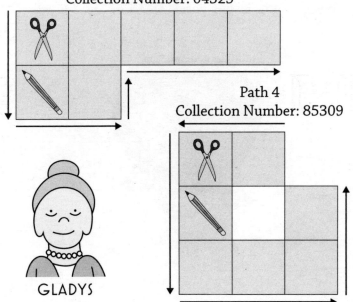

GLADYS

8. MISSING LINK

WITH THE LOCATIONS identified, it is time to investigate the location where each of the suspect's parcels were kept. Ben is about to ask the branch manager to lead the way when he notices her hesitate. Judging by her body language, Ben deduces that the manager is wary of letting them progress any further. On questioning, she says that no-one besides staff are normally allowed to access the rest of the post office, however she is willing to make an exception if they can help her solve a prize competition she's been struggling with in the local newspaper, reproduced here. Emily solves it quickly – can you do likewise?

Find the word that links the start and end word together to make two new words or phrases on each line, for instance TREE _ _ _ _ _ BOAT could be connected by the word 'house' to form the words 'treehouse' and 'houseboat'. Letters with a bold line underneath them will spell out the solution word. The first one has been filled in to get you started.

EMILY

Foot <u>R</u> <u>E</u> <u>S</u> <u>T</u> Mass

Life __ __ __ __ Distance

Down __ __ __ __ __ Boat

Ginger __ __ __ __ __ Winner

Finish __ __ __ __ Judge

Prim __ __ __ __ Water

Door __ __ __ __ Brother

Centre __ __ __ __ __ Coach

9. CIRCULAR LOGIC

EMILY hands back the puzzle and Audrey nods appreciatively. With a beckoning hand she encourages the group to follow her to a set of closed double doors. The team note that the doors have a thick chain wrapped around them with a lock preventing them from entering. Harold asks the branch manager to kindly open the lock so he may progress the investigation. Audrey scratches her head and closes her eyes in concentration. After a few moments she exhales in exasperation. It is clear that she has forgotten the code for the lock and it was never written down for security reasons. However, she remembers that there is a file that contains a clue to the code should this situation arise. Upon finding the section of the relevant file she is none the wiser and still cannot work out what the code is. Ben intervenes and calms Audrey, reassuring her that he will be able to work out the correct combination. Using the information below, can you help Ben figure out the combination to open the lock?

A black circle alongside a guess at the code indicates that a number in the guess is both correct and in the correct position. A grey circle indicates a correct number, but in the wrong position. The branch manager also remembers that no digit repeats within the code.

BEN

1458 ● ●

9083 ●

2136 ● ●

7831 ● ● ●

10. MIXED MESSAGE

AFTER ACCESSING the next room by deducing the combination for the lock, the team are keen to explore this location. They are in a massive room filled with rows of boxes on industrial shelving, various pieces of machinery and a mountainous pile of sacks containing letters and postcards. The branch manager leads the team to a particular shelf where a stack of papers with order forms and returns labels can be found. The group are quick to dismiss what they are shown (not spotting anything noteworthy within its contents) and are just about to cease searching when Ben uncovers a small note hidden underneath a pile of envelopes. He focuses hard on the contents before shrugging and passing it around the group. On the card is a bizarre language which is unrecognisable to the rest of the team. When the card reaches Emily, she studies its contents intently and asks Harold for assistance. She explains that she should be able to crack the code using her language skills and Harold's logical brain. Ben and Gladys wait patiently as half of the team dedicate themselves purely to the task at hand. Do you have what it takes to similarly crack the code and work out the contents of the mysterious notecard?

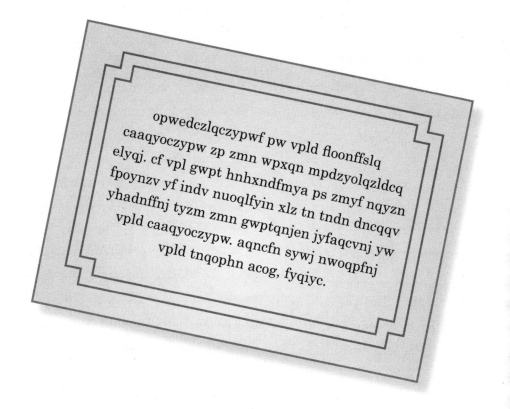

opwedczlqczypwf pw vpld floonffslq
caaqyoczypw zp zmn wpxqn mpdzyolqzldcq
elyqj. cf vpl gwpt hnhxndfmya ps zmyf nqyzn
fpoynzv yf indv nuoqlfyin xlz tn tndn dncqqv
yhadnffnj tyzm zmn gwptqnjen jyfaqcvnj yw
vpld caaqyoczypw. aqncfn sywj nwoqpfnj
vpld tnqophn acog, fyqiyc.

HAROLD

EMILY

11. ITEM NUMBER

WITH THE CONTENTS of one package identified, the team move to the second location in the hope of finding out more. At this location a pile of boxes have been stacked in a corner containing nothing but foam packaging. On further inspection, Gladys finds an order invoice left abandoned in one of the larger boxes. Emily notes that this box must have been here for a while judging purely by the fact it looks a little old and battered. Gladys scans through the invoice hoping to uncover some new information that will assist the team in their investigation, but all that she can spot is a series of order numbers. Ben decides to take a look for himself and peers over Gladys' shoulder, before manipulating the order numbers in various ways. Less than a minute later the duo confirm they know what the box contains, and the recipient of the order. Are you able to do the same?

BEN

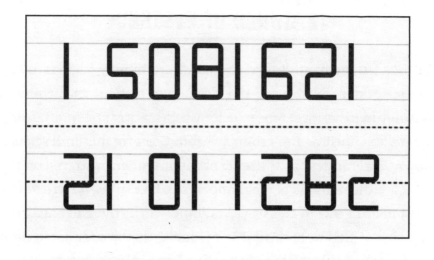

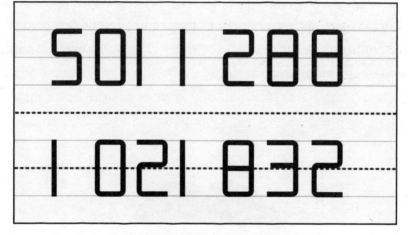

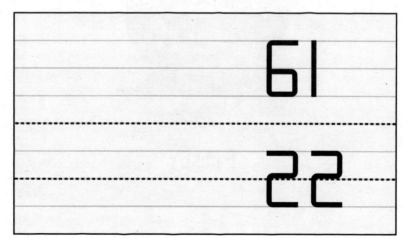

12. SHRED OF EVIDENCE

THE GANG are next directed to a desk containing various items of stationery. Examining the desk, Ben notices that there is nothing here besides some pencil stubs, a stack of sticky notes, and a shredder. Just as the group are about to give up, Emily bends down and empties the contents of the shredder. Scattered on the desk are the remains of what appears to be a message written by a supplier to one of the suspects. Emily expertly rearranges the remains of this note until it is readable, thus revealing an item (or items) a suspect has ordered. The rest of the team realise that Emily is treating these paper strips as a kind of jigsaw puzzle by reassembling the order of the columns. Are you able to decipher the message using this method?

EMILY

'	I	S	H	C	E	I	R
O	R	F	E	D		R	O
E	R	N	A	G	D	R	2
N	L	G	E	E	I	N	K
O		R	S	D	F	A	P
E	N	D	E	L	T	A	T
S	E	!	W	O	R	R	G

13. BEHIND BARS

THE BRANCH MANAGER leads the sleuthing group to some freestanding metal shelving containing boxes of all shapes and sizes. Most of the boxes are completely empty and devoid of any content, besides one. Harold grabs the box in question from the bottom shelf and presents a series of barcodes on the side of the box to the group. He also notices the name 'Andrew Gatlin' written above them which of course instantly piques the interest of the group. Analysing the barcodes, he comes to realise that they are actually an adaptation of a well-known code. Knowing that Emily would be a useful companion to help uncover the message, he invites her over to crack the conundrum. Soon the pair reveal the name of a magazine that they surmise Andrew has recently subscribed to. Use your code-breaking capabilities to find out the name of the publication.

HAROLD   EMILY

Andrew Gatlin

14. GOING PLACES

NOW THAT ALL the parcel contents have been recovered, and the owners of each parcel identified, Emily feels confident that another name can be eliminated from the suspect list. She states that Andrew can be eliminated as he has only just started gardening as a hobby. It is highly unlikely he would have the skills necessary to grow lily of the valley successfully in under a month AND know how to extract the necessary components to formulate the poison. The team respect that Andrew is showing an interest in a hobby that has brought much recognition to the family. They have, after all, become quite successful in the village Annual Horticultural Display. The rest of the suspects have been accepted into prestigious gardening clubs, have purchased expert equipment, and tropical foliage from overseas. These suspects appear to be much more competent gardeners. Andrew however is a novice given the title of the magazine he has subscribed to.

The team grin with satisfaction as their investigation has proven to be successful yet again. After conferring with each other, the sleuthing squad decide to ask the branch manager if they have any idea as to where the gardening enthusiasts of Little Riddlewood would be likely to meet. The branch manager shakes her head and explains how she is not a budding gardener herself so has no real idea where green-fingered residents would likely convene. Instead, she opens up a desk drawer and hands the team a map of the village that was concealed inside. The gang consult the map and notice how each landmark within the village is labelled in a strange order. Emily muses that perhaps there is something additionally embedded within this map that could help them: can you identify the next location the group of detecting dynamos should investigate?

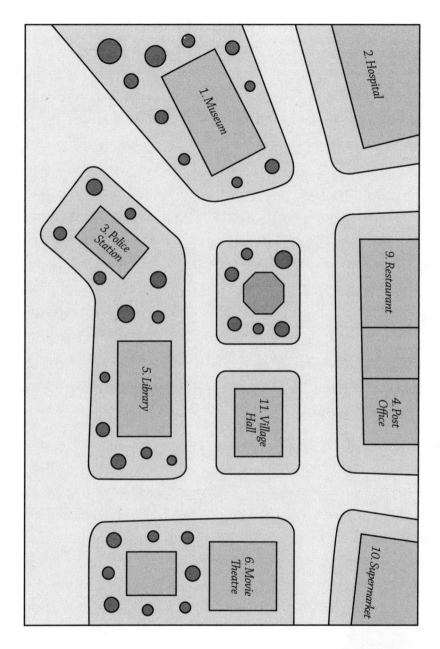

EMILY

SUMMARY

ARMED WITH the next location to investigate, the team excitedly exit the post office and bid farewell to the branch manager. As Ben, Emily and Gladys climb into the passenger seats of the car, they recap the events of the visit: most importantly they uncovered that many expert gardeners, growers and plant enthusiasts live in Little Riddlewood. This has allowed them to eliminate another person suspected of the murder of Mayor Malady. Harold sits in the driver's seat of the car and starts the ignition. This leads the rest of the team to recall the most unusual discovery of the investigation so far: Harold's aptitude at the operation of large machinery!

As Harold pulls away from the post office, the rest of the team sharpen their pencils and minds for what lays in store for them at the next location.

CHAPTER 5

DIGGING UP DIRT

1. MAKING AN ENTRANCE

AFTER a smooth journey towards the allotment, Harold steers the car down a dusty dirt path which cuts through the woods of Little Riddlewood. The team spot all kinds of wildflowers, fungi, and animals. Emily explains she had no idea that so many species of flora and fauna can be found in their local woodland. Ben agrees and adds how the presence of an allotment close by to this forest makes complete sense. There is no better location for it to exist. After all, inspiration is just a stone's throw away! With that, Harold stops the car. It appears that the team have almost arrived at their destination. Harold reveals that there is one problem, however. He knows that the members of the allotment are real sticklers for the rules and recalls a conversation that there is only one proper route to take to access the entrance to the allotment.

After several minutes of collective exploration, Emily points to three signs that have strange writing on them. She muses that perhaps they hint at the direction they should take. Harold begins jotting down his workings and uncovers the direction to the allotment entrance in mere minutes. Can you reveal the hidden messages within the signs and work out how to gain proper access to the next location?

HAROLD

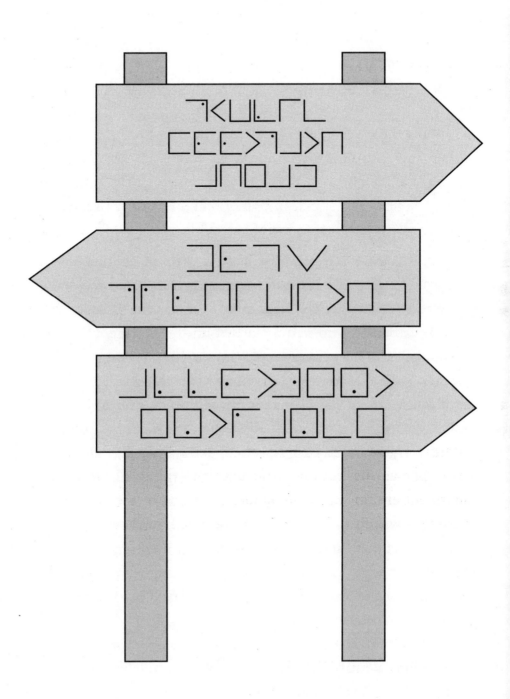

115

2. MISSING PERSON

AS THE TEAM enter the allotment after carefully deciphering the signs, they spot a familiar face amongst the vegetables: Inspector Pointer. As with their second meeting in the police station, his mouth is bent into a frown and his forehead is deeply furrowed. Assessing the scenery, Harold notices that there are many police officers investigating the area and even a forensics team retrieving evidence amongst plant pots. As they approach the esteemed detective, he breathes a deep sigh of relief. It is clear to see that the village's detective is in a spot of trouble.

Inspector Pointer explains how, like the team of sleuths, he has managed to eliminate another suspect. He had even come to the same conclusion that the remaining suspects are all avid (and skilled) gardeners who rent a plot within the allotment. He has assembled a team of officers to thoroughly investigate Little Riddlewood's allotment to gather any items that may have been used in the crime. The inspector himself was meant to join the search but has been left checking the sign-in sheet of the officers on duty. By analysing the sign-in sheet and by taking a head count of the officers currently investigating the allotment, he has deduced that there is one officer who has not reported for duty. The Inspector explains that a single path can be made in the grid from all the collar numbers of the police officers as seen in the number bank, which is created by moving from number to number either horizontally or vertically, and uses every number in the grid, starting at the highlighted grey number. There is only one collar number that is missing in the grid. He challenges Ben to help him identify the truant officer using this method. Can you find the collar number of the officer that has failed to turn up for their shift and thus should be disciplined?

6	1	4	8	8	7	7	6	8	2
5	7	2	2	6	0	1	2	3	5
1	5	6	6	1	5	1	4	4	2
9	2	7	7	5	6	4	2	5	7
4	1	3	7	5	6	8	6	6	9
4	2	4	3	8	4	6	1	7	6
8	9	4	5	0	2	5	5	2	2
2	4	1	1	5	4	8	7	2	0
3	8	0	4	9	5	7	7	9	4
2	4	3	4	3	2	1	5	8	2

12345, 41108, 42897, 43432, 46551, 48232, 49244, 50248, 51759, 52867, 53857, 56486, 57226, 60029, 65192, 66241, 67314, 72220, 75160, 76972, 78841

BEN

3. A ROSE BY ANY OTHER NAME

AFTER FINDING the number of the truant officer, the Inspector makes a brief call to the police station so that they can discipline the officer accordingly. Emily asks the Inspector if the team's arrival at the allotment would interfere with their investigation. In fact, the Inspector welcomes the extra (four) sets of hands and leads the group to a nearby plot of soil. He goes on to say how the officers have had trouble naming the plants in this location. As lily of the valley was used to murder Mayor Malady, it is imperative that every plant within the allotment is identified, especially as each of the suspects have a plot here. Inspector Pointer suspects that the words labelled on the plant stakes are a hint as to their real names. Are you able to uncover them?

EMILY

4. OUT OF ORDER

WHILST investigating the plots of soil surrounding the allotment, Gladys notices that three different plants have been labelled with the names of colours rather than anagrams. She asks the Inspector if his team have found any information relating to what the colours might mean. Unfortunately, he responds, his officers have yet to find anything that would help and, furthermore, he has little confidence in the capabilities of some of his colleagues. He explains that a team of his officers have moved the numbered markers attached to some of the items identified as potential evidence. Senior Officer Shrewd only has a series of statements that allude to the correct marker associated with each to work from. The Inspector leads the team over to the Senior Officer and introduces them, explaining that they will be able to help work out the correct marker that should be assigned to each item. The Senior Officer happily hands over the document to Harold and wishes him good luck. Are you similarly able to match each marker to the potential evidence by analysing each statement below? Evidence should be labelled 1-6.

- *The pieces of potential evidence that came in pairs had been assigned the highest and lowest markers.*

- *The flask was not positioned at a prime number.*

- *If the forensics team were working in numerical order, the trowel was processed before the flask but after the boots.*

- *Out of the remaining pieces of evidence, the footprint was positioned at the marker that was less than half of the value of the number assigned to the plant pot.*

HAROLD

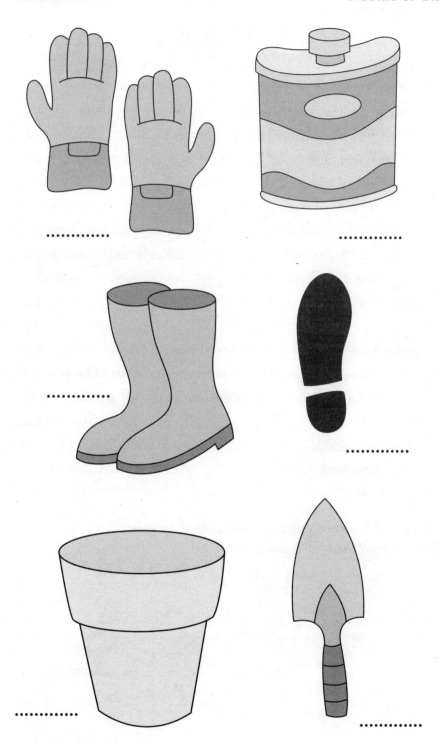

5. SPELLING BEE

THE TEAM begin their search of the allotment and they are at once drawn to the rhythmic buzzing of the bees that inhabit a nearby hive. Recalling that the suspect Callum Lozano took part in beekeeping as a hobby, Emily wonders if perhaps he left evidence around the area. As she approaches, Emily spies a note tacked to the side of the hive. Upon further inspection, the note is some sort of hexagonal puzzle. It appears that this puzzle is homemade, perhaps by Mr Lozano himself. Harold hypothesises that once the puzzle is solved it will reveal a word related to the case.

You must place the letters under the grid once each into the empty hexagons, in such a way as to both complete the grid and make it possible to find each of the words in the grid by moving from hexagon to adjacent hexagon. There is a hidden word to be extracted from the grid. Can you solve the puzzle and help progress the investigation?

EMILY   HAROLD

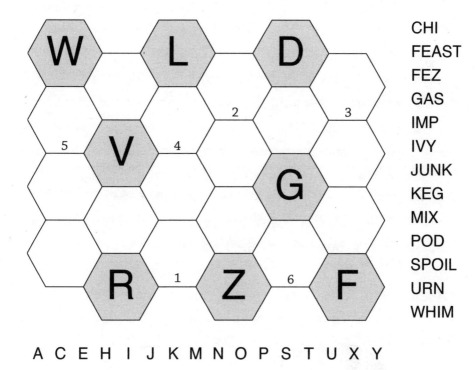

CHI
FEAST
FEZ
GAS
IMP
IVY
JUNK
KEG
MIX
POD
SPOIL
URN
WHIM

A C E H I J K M N O P S T U X Y

6. PEN PUSHER

EMILY informs the team of the word uncovered in the hexagonal puzzle. Ben mentions that upon entering the allotment he spotted a noticeboard. Perhaps that is what the puzzle is referring to?

The group make their way over to the noticeboard, being careful not to get in the way of busy forensic officers dusting for prints and swabbing for DNA, and they soon reach it. Many adverts are posted on the board intended to entice the skilled gardeners of the allotment into discounted gardening equipment, seeds and other related paraphernalia. Amongst these notices are missing posters for cherished pets, the allotment guidelines, and a sign-up sheet for the Annual Horticultural Display. Crucially, Harold spots that all three of the remaining suspects have signed up to show off their gardening capabilities at the Annual Horticultural Display. There is no doubting their skills now!

After a few minutes spent studying the contents of the notice-board, Emily work outs the next location in the allotment that they should investigate. Can you work out what it is?

EMILY

Annual Horticultural Display

Sign up here:

Silvia Taylor

Callum Lozano

Richie Meddit

_____

_____

_____

_____

50% OFF
ALL VEGETABLE SEEDS!

**At Little Riddlewood
Garden Centre**

ALLOTMENT GUIDELINES

1. Members must take care of the landscape.
2. Members must pay allotment rent or it will result in cancellation.
3. Meetings are scheduled on the first Thursday of the month.
4. Members must sign in and log their name and date.
5. Members must secure the allotment gate with the lock and chain.
6. Members must wear gloves and other protective wear for pruning.
7. Members are responsible for the treatment of pests and bugs.
8. Members must maintain cleanliness of their area out of common courtesy.
9. When using sharp tools, members must ensure they are always kept within sight.
10. Members must ensure all tools are returned.
11. Members must tend to all weeds.

ULTIMATE

7. OPENING NUMBER

MOVING swiftly to the next location, the gang predict that there will be a mountain of clues stashed within it. This theory is all but confirmed when they approach the door to find it is secured by a lock. Searching the area, Ben finds a slip of paper underneath a garden gnome. He unfolds it to reveal a sudoku which has not been filled in. The numbers that appear in the shaded diagonal must be the combination to the nine-digit potting shed lock. Are you able to uncover the code?

		3		4	7			
1			2				8	
						2		9
2			9			4		
		7			6			8
7		5						
	3				2			6
			4	6		1		

BEN

8. TABLE SCRAPS

THE TEAM bundle in and take stock of their surroundings. The building is almost filled to the brim! On one of the walls shelving has been built consisting of pigeonholes which hold some gardening items. Ben explains that the configuration of the shelves looks strangely familiar to him. He wonders if the specific pigeonhole that contains each item is somehow relevant. Harold adds that it appears far too random for it to be accidental. Why would there be so many pigeonholes with only a few items placed within them considering how full the shed is? Wouldn't the members of the allotment want to use all space available to them? The group conclude that another clue must be concealed here. Can you figure out what word the pigeonholes are holding?

BEN

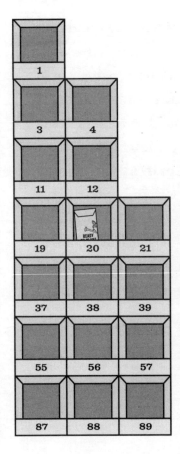

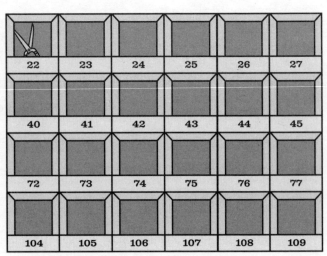

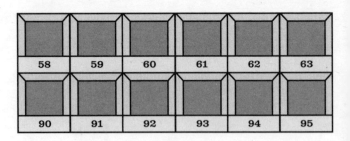

								2
			5	6	7	8	9	10
			13	14	15	16	17	18
28	29	30	31	32	33	34	35	36
46	47	48	49	50	51	52	53	54
78	79	80	81	82	83	84	85	86
110	111	112	113	114	115	116	117	118

64	65	66	67	68	69	70	71
96	97	98	99	100	101	102	103

9. TALL ORDER

AFTER solving the shelving unit conundrum, the group turn their attention to another wall of the building. Gladys spots a collection of oil cans messily lined up against the wall. Could the word that was hidden in the shelving unit be a subtle reference to this? Emily agrees it seems plausible and begins examining the layout of the cans. She suspects that, like the previous puzzle, another word is hidden within plain sight. Can you work out what it could be?

EMILY

10. PENCIL IN

GLADYS walks over to the next location and opens the doors. All that she can find is a battered puzzle book that has been bookmarked. Inspecting the area more closely, she notices that a poster is peeling away from the walls revealing something shiny and metallic underneath. She rips it off and discovers a safe that has been embedded at the back of the cupboard. It must have had a false back inserted! Ben notes that he is familiar with this model (being the treasurer for several clubs in the village) and announces that a four-digit code must be inputted using the keypad. Gladys says that no notes have been left that could assist them and she made sure to thoroughly inspect every inch of the surrounding area. She can't imagine that the bookmarked puzzle is not important somehow as the puzzle book is the only item that has been left in the cabinet. Ben agrees and suggests that perhaps solving the puzzle will supply some useful information.

Squares containing numbers indicate how many of the adjacent squares (including diagonally-adjacent squares) and the square itself must be shaded. Therefore a zero means that neither the square itself nor any of its neighbours are shaded, likewise a nine in a square means that the square itself and all eight neighbours are shaded. Can you solve the puzzle?

		3		3	2				0			0	0			
4				6				0								0
5		7	8	7		2							2			0
				4		5		5		1		1				
	3		6	3			6		5	3				6		
0							6	5						5		5
	3		6	3			3			6				3		6
0							5		6	5				5		
			7	2		5						3				3
	1		5			1				1	0			5		
		6		4			2	2			3				2	
3	6			3	0		0							5		0
	8						2	8						7		
1				0			3				2			4	2	
	3			0			0				7			3		
		3			1					5	6			4	2	
0		6			1									7		
1	7			3			3	4		3		5				3
		8			8	3						5		8	5	
3					6					4	4		5			

GLADYS

11. TOOLS FOR THE JOB

AFTER completing the puzzle and finding the next hint for the location of the safe code, Gladys turns to the wall which has many forms of gardening equipment resting against it. The rest of the team search for anything that could resemble numbers. Perhaps someone has etched something on the walls or hidden a note underneath the watering can? The gang search to no avail. After a few moments Emily suggests that the team simply step back and assess the situation at hand. She wonders if they aren't quite seeing the full picture. The group agree and walk across to the opposite side of the shed. At once Ben and Gladys spot the four-digit code. Are you able to do the same?

BEN   GLADYS

12. PLANT A SEED OF DOUBT

BEN inputs the code they have found using the safe keypad. As he presses ENTER on the safe's keypad, the green light on the front panel blinks. This is at once followed by a high-pitched BEEP. Success! Ben reaches into the safe and pulls out a grid littered with lily of the valley plants and a series of lily of the valley plants drawn at the bottom of the page. Harold suspects that this is a crucial clue to the investigation. The fact that lily of the valley flowers are present on the puzzle suggests that this relates to the murder of Mayor Malady. Especially considering it was locked away in a hidden safe!

Deduce the location in the grid of each of the ten lily of the valley plants listed: one plant occupies four consecutive squares, two plants occupy three consecutive squares, three plants occupy two consecutive squares and four plants occupy a single square. Numbers around the edge of the grid specify the number of plant segments found in each row and column of the grid. Each plant is surrounded on all sides (horizontally, vertically and diagonally) by empty squares. Using these rules, can you place all of the lily of the valley plants in the grid?

HAROLD

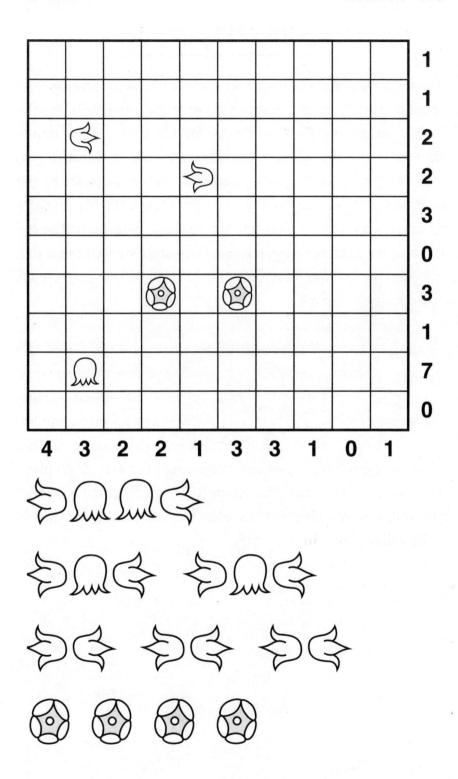

13. MAP OUT

HAROLD reaches into the safe once more and finds a map detailing the layout of the allotment as seen from above. The fact that nothing is obviously clear suggests that the murderer has intentionally added layers of security in case they are caught. They probably banked on the police's inability to solve the puzzles. How fortunate that Little Riddlewood's premier amateur sleuthing group are now involved in this investigation! What could the grid and map mean: is there something to be uncovered here?

HAROLD

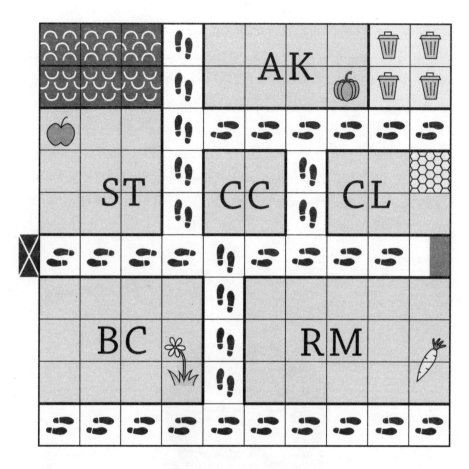

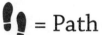 = Path   = Noticeboard

 = Entrance/exit   = Compost bins

 = Beehive   = Potting shed

14. REAP WHAT YOU SOW

EMILY decides to empty the safe to be sure that the team have not missed anything of note. Interestingly, she finds three different seed packets, shown here. There are planting instructions on each packet, and two columns of colours which have been handwritten. Emily's face lights up as she remembers that some plants in the allotment that were colour-coded have yet to be identified. Perhaps these seed packets hold the key to naming the plants and will additionally aid the police in their investigation. Can you figure out how to crack the code the seed packets hold?

EMILY

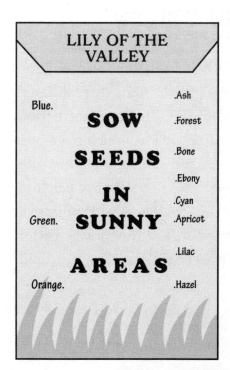

LILY OF THE VALLEY

Blue.

Green.

Orange.

SOW

SEEDS

IN

SUNNY

AREAS

.Ash

.Forest

.Bone

.Ebony

.Cyan

.Apricot

.Lilac

.Hazel

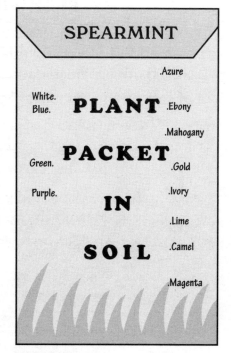

SPEARMINT

White.
Blue.

Green.

Purple.

PLANT

PACKET

IN

SOIL

.Azure

.Ebony

.Mahogany

.Gold

.Ivory

.Lime

.Camel

.Magenta

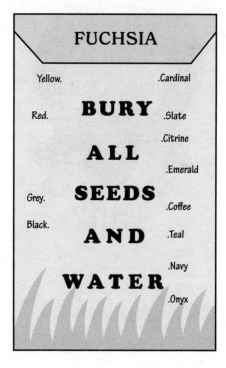

FUCHSIA

Yellow.

Red.

Grey.

Black.

BURY

ALL

SEEDS

AND

WATER

.Cardinal

.Slate

.Citrine

.Emerald

.Coffee

.Teal

.Navy

.Onyx

15. BUYING TIME

THE LAST ITEM Emily finds in the safe is a gardening catalogue which has been bookmarked at a particular page. The catalogue is out of date by a fair number of years and the company that had sent out the catalogue has long been out of business. In fact, this catalogue is advertising their closing sale. There is no reason for this catalogue to have been kept unless there is something hidden within it. The team confer and arrive at the conclusion that a clue must be hidden on the bookmarked page. Are you able to extract the word hidden on the page shown?

EMILY

EVERYTHING MUST GO!

Wheelbarrow

Item no. 87239

£5.10

A MASSIVE 90% REDUCTION!

Holds 460lbs of water!

Garden Fork

Item no. 65243

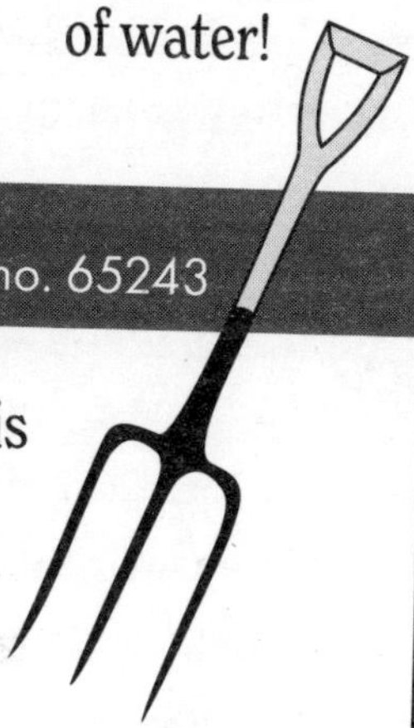

£6.04

This 3-pronged tool is perfect for digging up weeds!

Lawnmower Battery

Item no. 96264

40V

HOLDS A CHARGE OF UP TO 2 HOURS!

£6.04

Quick assembly in only 3 easy steps!

37

SUMMARY

BEN, Emily and Harold wonder what could be in London until Gladys informs them that the prices of each of the items coincidentally line up with train times to London from Little Riddlewood's station. She knows this as many times she has travelled to London to attend art galleries, openings, and private viewings. Often, she has travelled this early to make the most of the day. There must be a reason as to why this location was concealed and so the group decide that the next location to visit within the town will be Little Riddlewood's train station. Perhaps more information relating to the murder can be gleaned there.

As the gang make their way back through the allotment, they decide to inform Inspector Pointer of their next moves and to check the location of the lily of the valley plants. The Inspector is grateful for the information and the party of five inspect the plots of land labelled with coloured stakes once more. After confirming that the grid map location of the lily of the valley plants align with the placement of the coloured stakes, the Inspector beckons over the forensic team to take samples. As none of the lily of the valley plants were identified on Callum Lozano's plot of land within the allotment, the group (including Inspector Pointer) are confident that he should be eliminated as a suspect.

With that done, the team of amateur detectives bundle into Harold's vehicle. With only two more suspects in the running the case is approaching a conclusion. Will the murderer of Mayor Malady be named at the next location? With that question lingering in the air Harold starts the car and drives, once again, through Little Riddlewood's picturesque woods.

CHAPTER 6
KEEPING TRACK

1. WAVE THE FLAG

THE JOURNEY towards Little Riddlewood's train station is a picturesque one. The gang never seem to tire of the views that they can see from the car. As well as the usual wildlife, the group enjoy spying on their fellow inhabitants tending to their front gardens, chatting to their neighbours, and strolling through their quaint neighbourhood. It is hard to reconcile this with the despicable act that has been committed by either Richie Meddit or Silvia Taylor. Each member of the sleuthing squad recall having only had pleasant interactions with either party. Richie is very popular as the village doctor and Silvia always gives up her time for a chat (especially to discuss her books!) With that thought, Harold indicates left and turns into the car park of Little Riddlewood's train station. Who will be revealed as Mayor Malady's murderer?

The team make their way across the car park towards the train station entrance. Suddenly, Ben catches a glimpse of movement from the corner of his eye. He calls the group to his position and points a steady finger towards a woman in the near distance. She is waving a flag in each hand in a very particular pattern. Harold analyses the pattern configuration and concludes that she is trying to communicate something to the group. Gladys is of the impression that the woman must have heard about their investigation and that she is trying to point the team in the right direction. Can you work out the message?

GLADYS

2. WHISTLE STOP

NOW KNOWING who the team should contact at the train station, they head towards the main gate. Emily gently pushes on the gate which refuses to budge. Ben, Gladys, and Harold join in the effort but it is of no use: the gate is locked. Assessing the situation, Emily spots a number of notices and some whistles displayed in a glass-fronted box belonging to the conductors. Ben muses that perhaps a series of whistles need to be blown in a particular order to unlock the gate. Can you identify the series of notes that must be played to open the gate and enter the train station?

EMILY

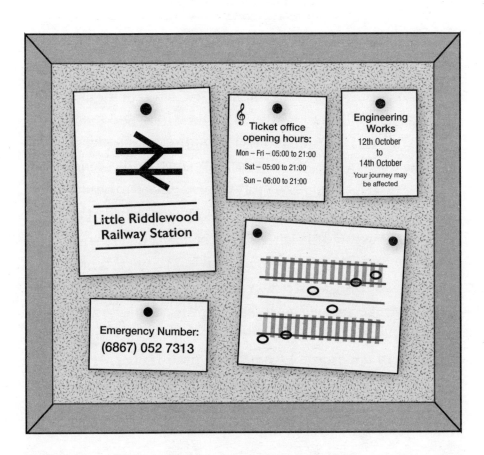

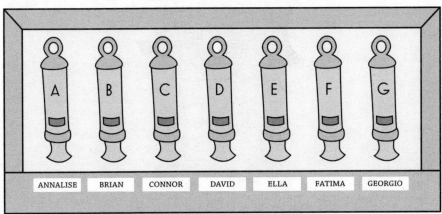

3. TRAIN OF THOUGHT

THE GANG make their way into the station and begin their investigation by attempting to assess which platform the train to London usually departs from. Ben walks over to the departure board displayed in the main foyer of the station but immediately notices that it is malfunctioning. The only thing that the board is showing is a few sporadic pixels! Harold strides over to a platform and assesses the train currently pulled up, then he quickly turns away and heads to another, then another, then another, final, platform. The team are baffled by this sudden burst of energy and Gladys explains how she has only seen Harold get this motivated when he is solving a particularly taxing puzzle. Within no time Harold has reconvened with the gang. He assures them that by just studying the side views of the trains in the platforms he has managed to determine each of their destinations. Harold had conveniently jotted down his findings in his trusty notebook to show the gang. Can you determine the destination of each train by analysing each window drawn by Harold?

HAROLD

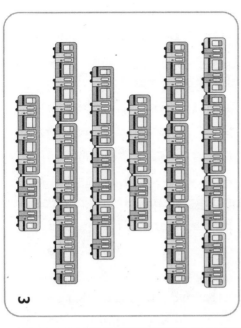

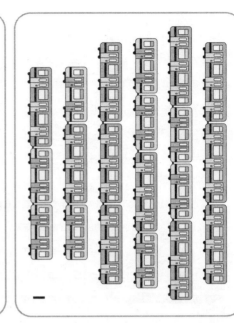

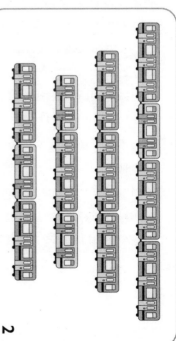

4. ALL ON SCHEDULE?

THE TEAM are impressed with Harold's capabilities and now, armed with the correct platform to investigate, search for the conductor on duty as hinted at by the woman with the flags. They, unsurprisingly, find him sitting at the station's information desk. After briefly explaining their situation the employee begins to shuffle the various papers on his desk. He asserts that usually the station is much cleaner than today, but they are having some issues with their internal systems. Harold nods and gestures to the departure board. He mentions to the group that this fact must explain the departure board error! Emily makes it clear that the team would like to see the logs of the recent early morning departures from platform 3. The conductor's eyes widen at the mention of that platform number. He mentions that only the train Turbo had passengers which fit the description of the murder suspects. With a swift hand motion the employee presents a piece of paper with a series of codes written on it. He explains that all the relevant information regarding the platform is contained on the piece of paper. If the team are as capable as they say, then it should be no trouble for them to decipher the message. If they are able to do that, then the employee can help confirm if the suspects were ever on the train to begin with. The team study the relevant section of the logbook and get cracking. Are you up to the challenge?

— LOGBOOK —			
ENGINE	**DRIVER**	**STATUS**	**COMMENTS**
HDRUG	NZFIRXV	XZMXVOOVW	ZOO KZHHVMTVIH IVRNYFIHVW
IZKRW	SZIIB	WVOZBVW	VMTRMVVIH XZOOVW
YIRHP	ERXGLI	UZFOGB	YLLPVW ULI HVIERXV
GFIYL	UIVBZ	ZIIREVW	ZOO KZHHVMTVIH KIVHVMG

HAROLD

5. WAITING GAME

WITH THE LOG successfully decoded the team speak once again to the conductor on duty. He seems very impressed with their efforts and rewards them with a short clap. Then, he retrieves a set of keys from his trouser pocket alongside a folded piece of paper. He explains that he needs to search the information desk for the receipts from the relevant journey to London. In the meantime, the amateur sleuths can let themselves into the locked waiting room to pass the time. He explains that the key to the waiting room is the one that slots perfectly into the lock mechanism as printed on the folded paper. It is down to the team to work out which key out of the selection provided is the correct one to unlock the door. Gladys studies the image and the keys intently and has an answer within a minute. Are you able to do the same?

GLADYS

A

B

C

D

E

F

G

H

6. ALL ABOARD

AFTER being in the waiting room for around 10 minutes (taking a well-deserved rest) the station employee returns with a number of ticket receipts in hand. He explains that their appearance mimics that of the standard tickets purchased by customers, but that these are the copies that the station keeps for their own records, much like a receipt. The gang study each ticket and are confused by the fact that none of the tickets explicitly state the name of the purchaser. The employee giggles and the team can't seem to understand the joke. He apologises and begins to explain that the station uses a very particular method to note who buys each ticket. He states that he was not laughing at them but merely at the fact that he forgot the system is not immediately obvious to outsiders as it is second nature to him. He challenges Harold and Gladys to figure out this quirk that allows station employees to determine the recipient of each ticket. Can you identify which of the selection of tickets belong to Richie Meddit and Silvia Taylor respectively?

HAROLD   GLADYS

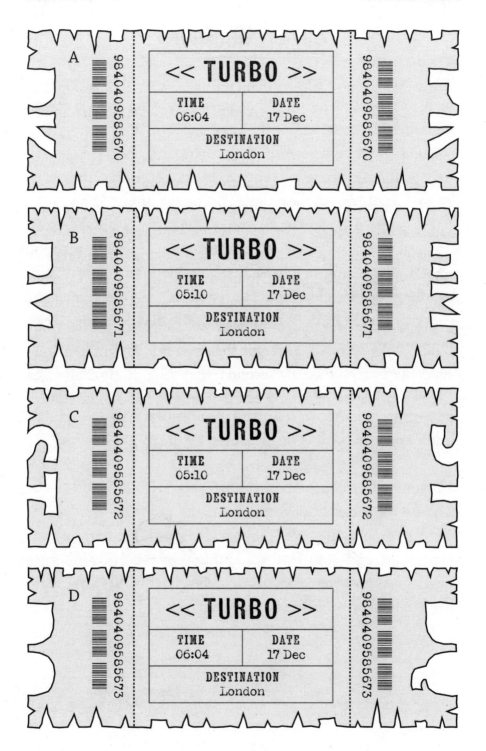

7. MAKING TRACKS

IT SEEMS THAT both Richie Meddit and Silvia Taylor were on the 5:10 train to London! What was it that they both travelled there for? The members of the gang each privately ponder this question and decide to continue investigating the train station. Perhaps there is more evidence to be gathered that they have yet to encounter. As they all get up to exit the waiting room, Gladys spots a noticeboard with various flyers pinned to it. Amongst them are a list of furniture items for sale, a young woman advertising her babysitting services and information regarding the intended expansion of the train line commencing from this very station. Unfortunately, the details of the track's route are missing. Perhaps this is a lead the team can follow? Harold scans the map of the village and comes to the conclusion that he will be able to reconstruct the path of the track. Can you follow Harold's logic and identify the area of the village of Little Riddlewood that would be destroyed by the proposed plan?

Can you deduce the path of the new track from A to B in the diagram on the next page to reveal the proposed new route? Numbers around the edge of the grid indicate how many sections of track are placed in each row/column of the grid. The track cannot cross itself, and if it visits a square, it either passes straight through it or turns at a right angle inside it.

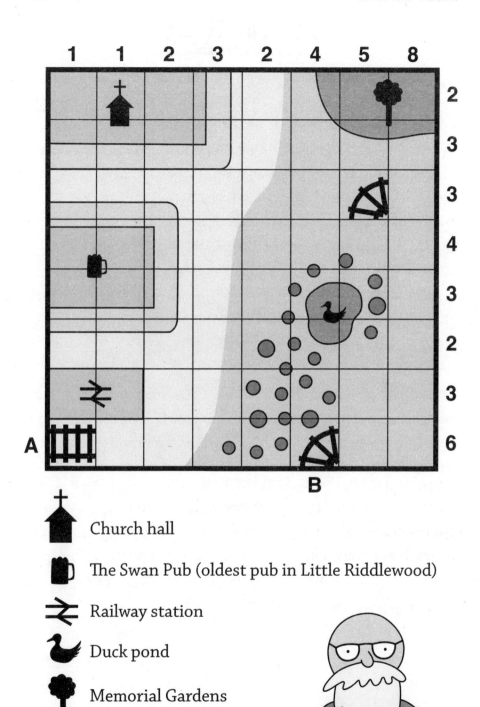

1   1   2   3   2   4   5   8

2
3
3
4
3
2
3
6

A

B

 Church hall

The Swan Pub (oldest pub in Little Riddlewood)

Railway station

Duck pond

Memorial Gardens

Woodland

HAROLD

8. GET THE MESSAGE

THE GROUP suspect that the planned works would definitely rub up some inhabitants of Little Riddlewood the wrong way. Looking back at their visit to the village hall, Ben recalls that Michael received a complaint regarding the expansion of the railway. He states that, in fact, they all viewed the relevant village hall meeting minutes. Gladys concurs and remembers that Silvia's full name was extracted from the transcript. She obviously was opposed to this expansion alongside a few other council members, yet her name was the only one that was purposefully concealed. The group turn to each other and agree that Silvia is now the lead suspect in the investigation. However, what does this have to do with Mayor Malady?

Our sleuthing squad decide to scan the station for any more information relating to the proposal. On the far side of the foyer the team encounter a stall which has various flyers and promotional material explaining the benefits that the planned works will have on the village. As well as increasing access to Little Riddlewood, it also promises more industry, jobs and tourism. Who is the lead figure endorsing this expansion, who has signed every piece of promotional material, and whose cardboard cutout is standing proudly next to the stall? None other than Little Riddlewood's late Mayor Malady!

On the stall the gang spot a suggestion box intended for comments on the campaign. Emily proposes that the team take a look at the contents. She opens the box and sorts through the positive and negative comments. Amongst the papers, she observes one note that has a completely different format. In fact, it is constructed exactly like a ransom note. Unfortunately, it has not been signed so the author is unknown. This, of course, was not unexpected but would have been a welcome addition! On first look, the message looks fairly straightforward but she concludes that there is another message hidden within its contents. Can you work out what it is?

to the Greedy mAyor Malady,

i am sickened By your intention to destroy the Land of little riddleWood. I must now cHoose Drastic action. Ensure you heed this wArning or face my wraTH.

EMILY

9. BAD NEWS

WHILST THE REST of the team comb through the remainder of the comments in the suggestion box, Harold notices a stand containing free local newspapers that are available to passengers to read on their train journeys. He scoffs as he notices that the top newspaper has been printed so poorly that the text is indecipherable. He lifts up the first copy and removes the only remaining newspaper on the stand. The quality is just as bad! The newspapers are dated 'Friday 2nd December' which is a couple of weeks out of date. The train station must have cancelled their order due to the printing error on this batch of newspapers. Emily strolls over to Harold and begins to inspect his discovery. Something on the front page has caught her eye. She holds out the two newspapers in each hand and shakes her head fiercely. Harold suspects that there is something that Emily has noticed that may help with their investigation. Can you work out what it is?

EMILY

Little Riddlewood Gazette

LITTLE RIDDLEWOOD, FRIDAY 2ND DECEMBER

WHERE: MAYOR MALADY'S MANOR
WHEN: MONDAY

Little Riddlewood Gazette

LITTLE RIDDLEWOOD, FRIDAY 2ND DECEMBER

WHERE: MAYOR MALADY'S MANOR
WHEN: MONDAY

10. SIGN ON THE DOTTED LINE

HAROLD and Emily have concluded that there was a protest at Mayor Malady's mansion before his murder. This would have given the culprit ample chance to study the mansion and plan their crime accordingly! The duo discuss their findings with Ben and Gladys and the group decide to investigate the railway expansion further.

After a few minutes poring through the various flyers and other documents, Ben identifies a petition in favour of the expansion of the railway. The group ask him to read out the names listed on the petition but he hesitates when he realises that it has all been written in code. Harold isn't particularly surprised. He describes how he too would conceal his name if he knew how polarising the proposal was. Ben hands over the petition to Emily in the hope that she can easily decode the contents. Are you able to use your code-breaking skills to do the same?

EMILY

RAILWAY EXPANSION PETITION

TQPCNF OWTRJA
UKGPPC VWTPGT
LWNKC MGTTA
TQDGTV YKNUQP
ENCWFKC NCYUQP
TCPFCNN OQTTKU
UKNXKC VCANQT

11. BRICK BY BRICK

SILVIA TAYLOR is listed as being in favour of the expansion! She has signed the petition! The reality of the situation dawns upon the team as they collectively realise that she must have changed her position after the village hall meeting and so is not the murderer. With this information, there is only one suspect remaining in the investigation into the murder of Mayor Malady. Gladys wanders away from the team to study a faded photograph hung on the wall of the train station foyer. The picture is situated next to a brochure stand advertising various activities that tourists can participate in in the village. Clearly, something has caught Gladys' attention and shortly a smile creeps across her face. It appears to the rest of the team that a couple of dots have been mentally connected in her brain regarding the case. The amateur detectives walk over to Gladys' position and study the image. It depicts a lovely scene of Little Riddlewood's memorial garden lush with flora. Included in the picture is a statue depicting what is assumed to be a prominent person from the village. Neither Ben, Emily, or Harold know who this person is as the statue's plaque fails to include her name. Gladys turns to the group and reveals that she has uncovered the identity and that it has been cleverly disguised. Can you do the same?

GLADYS

MEMORIAL GARDENS

12. SPELL IT OUT

IS THE LADY depicted in the statue related to Richie in some way? Surely it is no coincidence that she is holding a lily which is the very genus of plant used to murder Mayor Malady? The team turn these questions around in their heads in the hope that if they ruminate enough an answer will simply conjure itself into existence. Knowing that to be a futile endeavour, Emily eventually pores through the contents of the pamphlet stand and searches for a leaflet advertising the memorial gardens. A minute passes and she is successful! The team examine the contents of the pamphlet in the hope of discovering more about this landmark. The pamphlet contains more than meets the eye, however. Can you work out the message that is hidden within the text?

EMILY

Memorial Gardens

D1
U3

**Visit Little Riddlewood's prestigious Memorial Gardens! Free Entry!
Donations welcome!**

B4
T6
F9
D13
G15
R15
F17
O17
O19
T20
F21
M21
N24
A25
V26
R25
U26
C28
H29
L32

Little Riddlewood's Memorial Gardens have been preserved for
generations by the Meddit family who are local to the area. Marion
Meddit brought fame to this quaint village after her horticultural
skills consistently earned her the title of Britain's Best Lily Breeder.
In fact, in London, where the National Floral Guild is based, an
award has been made championing her knowledge which is only
offered to those who have dedicated their lives to the preservation
and celebration of the natural world. This is titled the Diamond Merit
which is an anagram of Marion's full name.

Throughout her life, Marion dedicated herself to the village and
helped maintain the appearance of public areas to much
appreciation. Whilst she remained renowned throughout her life, in
death her name slowly began to lose its relevancy as the generations
passed.

The Memorial Gardens are now the only remaining monument that
immortalise Marion's contribution to her village and champions her
membership of the horticultural community. The Meddit family
continue to pay their respects by visiting the home of the Diamond
Merit Award in the hope that the National Floral Guild never
disregard the origin of the famed achievement.

13. PROTECT THE PERIMETER

THIS CONFIRMS IT! Richie's relationship to Marion has been revealed and his motive for murdering Mayor Malady lies plainly in the pamphlet's text. He must have used lily of the valley to honour his ancestor and in retaliation for the planned destruction of the memorial gardens. His protest outside Mayor Malady's mansion allowed him to study the property and plan his crime. The pieces slot together for the group and they acknowledge that Inspector Pointer should be called immediately regarding this development. Harold rushes to the information desk and requests that the Inspector is contacted and told to meet them at Little Riddlewood station.

Half an hour passes and Inspector Pointer, with officers in tow, arrives at the station. As travelling by train is one of the quickest ways to depart the village it is imperative that it is kept guarded. Richie may try and escape at any moment, especially if he catches wind of the fact that he has been identified as the culprit! Knowing this, and knowing Harold used to be a police officer, Inspector Pointer requests that Harold help him assign officers throughout the station so that if Richie were to enter his capture would be guaranteed. Inspector Pointer hands the team a plan of the station. Can you place two officers, represented by 🛡 in each row, column and bold-lined region that constitute the grid? Officers cannot be in touching squares, not even diagonally!

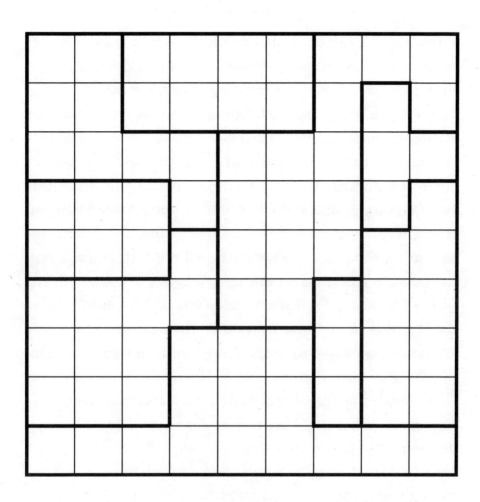

HAROLD

SUMMARY

THE GANG are hot on the heels of Richie Meddit, accompanied by the esteemed Inspector Pointer. Who would have thought that the respected village doctor would be the person to murder Little Riddlewood's mayor? During their visit to the train station the group have managed to establish Richie's motive. He resented that the proposed plan would destroy his beloved ancestor's statue in the memorial gardens. He must have been especially bitter about the fact that Marion Meddit remains largely forgotten within the community when she contributed so much. Richie used the lily of the valley plant, a flower type that she was renowned for breeding, as a way to honour his late relative. Similarly, his trip to London was made in order to go to the National Floral Guild and remind them of the contribution his family had made to horticulture. Through this scandalous murder the Meddit name will be known forever. The gang contemplate their findings as Harold drives them to the Meddit household. What could lay in wait for them there: danger or discovery?

CHAPTER 7

CLOSING IN

1. FOOT IN THE DOOR

THERE IS PALPABLE tension in the air as Harold drives the rest of the gang, alongside Inspector Pointer, to Richie Meddit's residence. Now that they have eliminated every other suspect, the gang are almost certain that Dr Meddit is the murderer. The gang believe that more evidence can be found at his house and so Inspector Pointer has arranged a warrant to search his property. The sleuthing squad feel certain that they are closing in on Mayor Malady's murderer.

Harold pulls into Richie's street and the team scramble out of the car. Inspector Pointer retrieves the warrant from his files and shakes his head. It appears that for the warrant to be validated he must enter in a house number. Unfortunately, Dr Meddit's house does not have a number on its front door. Ben analyses the rest of the houses along the road and concludes that all the door numbers along Richie's side of the road follow a specific pattern. By studying the other houses, and thus determining the pattern, Ben is able to identify Dr Meddit's house number. Can you do the same?

BEN

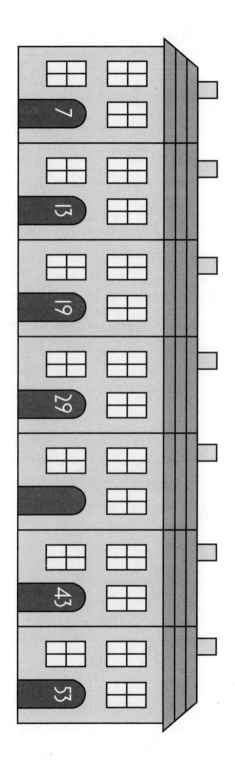

2. FOOD FOR THOUGHT

NOW THAT THE WARRANT has been correctly filled in there is nothing stopping the team from entering Richie Meddit's property. The gang share a determined glance before Inspector Pointer expertly manipulates the lock until the door opens with a foreboding creak.

The house is eerily silent and after a few minutes of looking in each room, the gang realise that Richie appears not to be at home. Inspector Pointer has given them free rein to explore and gather more evidence. Emily makes her way to the kitchen and notices something quite peculiar about the fridge door. Within a few moments she whispers six letters to herself, and in short order identifies a type of wine. Are you able to determine what it is?

EMILY

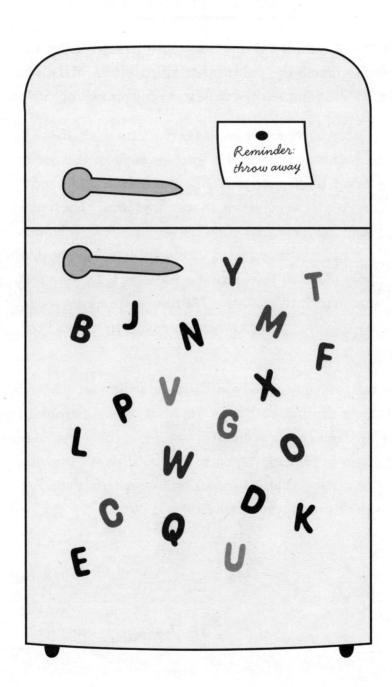

3. OUT OF DATE

THE NOTE 'Reminder: throw away' must be referencing the fact that Richie mixed the poison that killed Mayor Malady into a bottle of Shiraz and wanted to destroy any remaining evidence.

After a brief search, Emily manages to locate the half-full bottle of wine at the very back of a kitchen cupboard: it looks like Richie forgot to dispose of it! She retrieves it and hands it to Inspector Pointer as evidence. In another room of the house Ben is analysing the various pictures hung on the wall. It is apparent that Dr Meddit is very proud of his ancestry. Every photo is of a family member celebrating a life event. No-one features more prominently than Marion Meddit. There are also countless faded newspaper clippings celebrating her various horticultural projects.

Ben enters the hallway, and spots a calendar pinned to the wall. He briefly flicks through each page and whilst the numerous images of gardens and cottages are very ordinary, there is something particularly interesting taped to the back page. Studying the note, Ben can see that it is pointing to a specific date. Are you able to identify what that date is?

28th February – 118

BEN

4. STEP IN THE RIGHT DIRECTION

BEN recalls that this was an important date but can't quite recollect the reason. He reconvenes with the group and Emily explains how that was the date that Richie collected his package from the post office. The fact he felt the need to hide and disguise this date suggests that the items that he collected did, indeed, connect to the crime. The team split up once again and continue their investigation in Richie Meddit's residence.

Gladys and Harold, whilst searching the dining room, happen upon a pinboard containing another clue. It shows an image of the front of the garden shed and some writing is scrawled on the page next to it. Knowing that Richie is incredibly skilled at gardening and would most likely spend lots of his free time in the garden, Gladys, with Harold closely behind, makes her way out into the garden. They both immediately spot the shed. Gladys suspects that Dr Meddit has buried something in the ground as, after surveying the area, nothing jumps out at her as being unusual. Standing directly in front of the shed with her back to it, Gladys reads out the note:

"Take five paces north, then three paces west. Continue with three more paces west. Take four paces south, two east, four north, three east, two south then six west. Finally, take three paces south, and stop."

In which direction, and how many paces, must Gladys and Harold walk in order to stand at the spot where Richie buried something?

HAROLD

GLADYS

5. THOUGHT EXPERIMENT

GLADYS and Harold manage to locate a shovel propped up against the garden fence. Although the duo do not possess the strength that they did in their youth, propelled by adrenaline, they are able to dig a hole and retrieve a large chest from the earth below. Inside it are a set of clothes that, although crumpled, seem to be unstained. Harold concludes that this must be the set of clothes that Richie wore when he poisoned Mayor Malady. Why else would they need to be concealed? Gladys agrees and promptly calls Inspector Pointer from inside the house. He gathers the evidence and the pair return to their search.

Meanwhile, Ben has encountered a chemistry set within the spare room of the property. He notices a series of beakers, a Bunsen burner, a test tube rack and test tubes that have been labelled in a particular way. Harold enters and the pair try to determine what exactly Richie Meddit was formulating. Are you able to identify the substance?

HAROLD   BEN

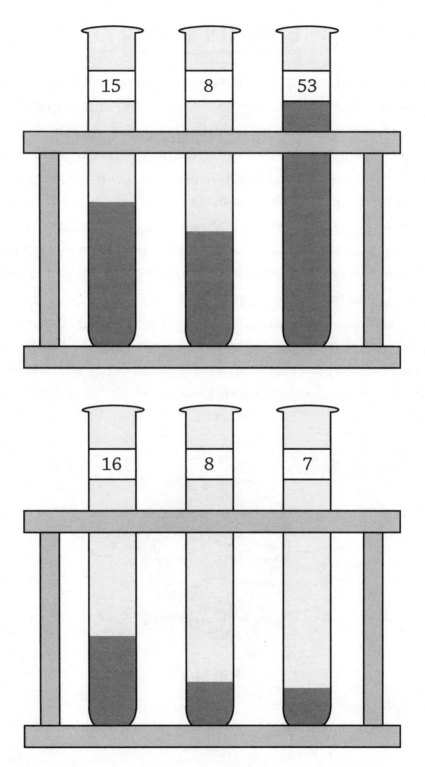

6. WRITER'S BLOCK

WHILST THE MEN determine that Richie was formulating poison upstairs, Emily investigates Dr Meddit's office space. She is instantly drawn to the desk that is littered with all kinds of debris. Amongst the mess Emily notices a pair of scissors, glue, tweezers and numerous copies of magazines with letters cut out of them. Emily smirks as she realises that this must be where Richie was constructing his threatening ransom-style notes. Her eyes are then drawn to a well-maintained typewriter that is situated on the desk. There is a sheet of paper trapped around the cylinder with a message printed on it. The page is riddled with errors and after studying the page for a few moments, Emily concludes that two pairs of letters have been switched with each other on the typewriter. Are you able to determine which letters these are by analysing the text shown here?

EMILY

1. ENSTOLL PONEC RAAM OND BUY SUPPLEIS FAR ET

2. DISTRAY IVEDINCI THRAUGHAUT LETTLI REDDLIWAAD

3. INSURI THI SELINCI AF WETNISSIS TA CREMENOL OCTEVETY

4. INCADI NATIS ORAUND HAUSI

5. BURY TAALS OND ATHIR RILOTID MOTIREOLS

6. SIT LACKS TA PONEC RAAM

7. BAAK PLONI TECKITS UNDIR OLEOS

8. LACK SILF EN HEDDIN PONEC RAAM UNTEL ENVISTEGOTEAN RUNS CALD

7. POINT THE FINGER

CLEARLY, Richie was only somewhat successful in his plan as the group still managed to identify him!

Emily realises that a perfect fingerprint can be extracted from the typewriter keys. There are numerous keys that Richie would have pressed that are perfectly sized to offer a complete print. She calls downstairs to Inspector Pointer and Gladys who then promptly make their way to the office. The inspector expertly retrieves a print from one of the typewriter keys and pulls out a file from his briefcase. He explains that he now needs to compare this print to the unidentified prints that were collected at the crime scene. Below are a series of unidentified prints from the manor. Can you identify which one exactly matches the sample taken from the typewriter?

GLADYS

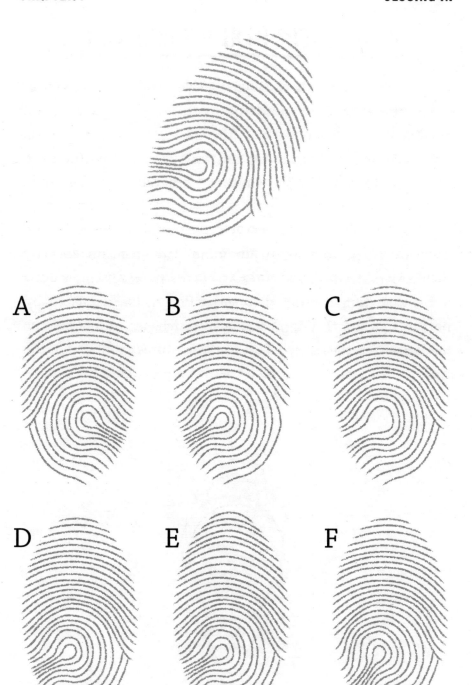

8. ALL THERE IN BLACK AND WHITE

INSPECTOR POINTER consults his files and determines that the print that has been matched with Richie Meddit's was found on Mayor Malady's corkscrew, the wine glasses found on the side-table next to the mayor, and various door handles across the property. Many of these rooms were out of bounds to the public.

The trio of Inspector Pointer, Emily and Gladys continue to search Richie Meddit's desk and come across an invoice listing various items that he had ordered to assist him in his crime. Gladys notices that another item has been purchased and cryptically hidden within the receipt. Can you work out what it is?

GLADYS

LOTSA STUFF

42-46 Main Street
Little Riddlewood
RW27 JAA

* *

CASH RECEIPT

* *

1 x Rubber Gloves	£2.00
1 x Protective glasses	£7.50
1 x Apron	£10.00
1x Chemistry set	£12.95
2 x Industrial detergent	£5.00
3 x Scourers	£3.00
1 x Pipette set	£9.99

* *

Total   **50.44**

* *

THANK YOU!

9. NOTE TO SELF

THE SUBGROUP bound over to meet with Ben and Harold to inform them that Richie Meddit has installed a panic room somewhere on his property. Shocked, but determined to gather any remaining evidence, the pair suggest that they should keep an eye out for any suspicious latches or locks that may be the access point to the panic room. Richie could be hiding within the panic room, or be out in Little Riddlewood somewhere following his plan. The group decide to prioritise obtaining any more evidence that could be hiding in plain sight that Richie may destroy if he gets a chance. The gang wonder what could be in the panic room. Will it be more evidence or Richie Meddit himself?

Emily, whilst searching the bedroom, comes across another sticky note stuffed in-between two pages of a book on his bedside table. Dr Meddit has been using this note as a bookmark. Emily observes some writing that has been jotted on the sticky note. At first, she thinks her vision is compromised but gradually realises that the message has been deliberately encoded. It must say something important if Richie went to the trouble of disguising it. Are you able to crack the code?

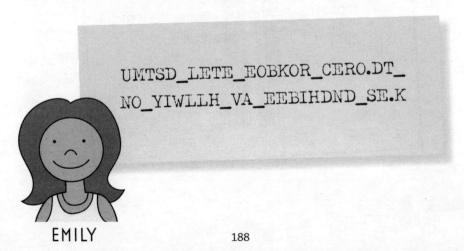

UMTSD_LETE_EOBKOR_CERO.DT_
NO_YIWLLH_VA_EEBIHDND_SE.K

EMILY   188

10. ZERO IN

WHILST INVESTIGATING the rest of the bedroom, the group find a hidden planner underneath Richie's mattress. Their eyes widen in anticipation. It is apparent that something must be contained within the planner that Richie wished to be kept away from prying eyes. With a steady hand, Ben flicks through the pages and lands on a spread littered with zeros and ones. The ladies of the group wonder what it could mean, but Ben and Harold are already translating the pages' contents into plain English. Are you able to figure out how to transform the text that has been concealed?

00010,10010,01001,01110,00111, 10000, 01111,
01001,10011,01111,01110,00101,00100, 00010,
01111,10100,10100,01100,00101, 01111,00110,
10011,01000,01001,10010,00001,11010, 10100,
01111, 01101,00101,00101,10100,
01001,01110,00111, 10111,01001,10100,01000,
01101,00001,11001,01111,10010, 00001,01110,
00100, 00110,00101,01001,00111,01110,
01001,01100,01100,01110,00101,10011,10011,
00001,10011, 00001,01110, 00101,11000,00011,
10101,10011,00101, 01110,01111,10100, 10100,
01111, 00100,10010,01001,01110,01011

HAROLD

BEN

11. ONE LAST WORD

THE GANG make their way downstairs, and, once they turn to go through the hallway, Emily notices a very odd panel that displays words lit by various lights and a keypad on the door to the cupboard under the stairs. She realises that this must be the entrance to Dr Meddit's panic room. It is clear that an additional word must be inputted to access the room, and Emily gets to work tackling the final word. Can you determine what the password is to gain access to the panic room? A black square indicates that the letter appears in the answer word in the same position, whilst a grey square indicates the letter appears in the answer word but in a different position. If the square has a white background, it means the letter does not appear in the answer word at all. No letter repeats in the answer word.

EMILY

S	H	O	W	Y
M	E	A	L	S
G	R	I	P	S
T	O	N	G	S

12. CUFF 'EM!

SUCCESS – the door unlocks! As it swings open they hear movement and quickly realise Richie Meddit is inside the room. He frantically gathers various papers, ready to try to push past the team and make his escape. The team instantly react and guard the entrance as the murderer tries without success to barge them out of the way. Inspector Pointer expertly manoeuvres Richie into handcuffs and speaks a series of numbers into his walkie talkie. Richie struggles at first but then realises he cannot escape. Can you crack Inspector Pointer's message?

576 423 21 611 18 41 67 32 31 22 333
53741 616327 645 795 1 1971 14 786 9113
31 32 63234 1 576 4644 14 775 6554 231 9213
3528 8921 53 14 332122 8562 1827 13 221
311391 78 411 634 1 354931 12561 4815 49 1
93 1 22 6289 . 5776 276 29145 17 1 589 41 965
413 41 42129 72 61 26 929 569 69 19332 23
49 1 18 4541 8731 36 66 41 914 299.

INSPECTOR POINTER

EPILOGUE

AFTER RICHIE MEDDIT'S arrest for the murder of Mayor Malady the village of Little Riddlewood received a considerable amount of publicity. The local gazette reported upon the case and followed Dr Meddit's trial closely. National newspapers also picked up on the story and updates on the trial even appeared on the evening news. A certain well-known news reporter particularly played on the juxtaposition of a sleepy well-heeled village experiencing a gruesome murder.

Inspector Pointer, and the rest of the local police officers, managed to gather enough evidence to convict Dr Meddit of murder: in no small part due to the efforts of Ben, Emily, Gladys and Harold. Due to the nature of the crime, and how it was solved, Little Riddlewood had an unprecedented boom in tourism. This was aided by the opening of the planned railway line expansion that Richie Meddit opposed. People from all over the country swarmed to visit the locations that our four amateur sleuths stopped at to investigate. Tony, the local librarian, had never had so many books about mysteries, conundrums and riddles checked out of the shelves!

Marion Meddit's statue was removed before the memorial gardens were demolished and was relocated to the village square. Although Richie committed a despicable act, notionally in the name of protecting his family's legacy, the village councillors (who were appointed after another election) felt that Marion

Meddit's contributions to the horticulture and community of Little Riddlewood should still be honoured at a local awards ceremony.

Amongst the honourees at the ceremony were Ben, Emily, Gladys and Harold. After their involvement with the case and the apprehension of the killer, the group were given awards acknowledging their stellar contribution to the community. The team now undertake far less dangerous endeavours, but enjoy gathering together to solve a weekly conundrum that still stumps even the best puzzle solvers: the Little Riddlewood Gazette cryptic crossword!

HAROLD   GLADYS

EMILY   BEN

SOLUTIONS

1. SET THE SCENE

2. KILLING TIME

Convert the entries on the notebook to numbers to reveal the three times: 13:52, 8:24, 5:50.

3. NAME THE DAY

Convert the dates that contain a symbol to letters (e.g. 1=A) and form an anagram of these, to reveal the answer JUDITH. Thanks to Harold's perception skills, the group now have another person to add to their list of suspects.

4. CRIMINAL RECORD

Take the numbers from each record's timestamp and use that as an indicator as to what letter to extract from the name on each record. For example, the timestamp 03:09 indicates you should take the 3rd letter and 9th letter in the name Michael Jackson which leaves you with C and A. When all the letters are extracted the name CALLUM is created.

5. COMPARE NOTES

The answer is ANDREW. The second piece of paper is the only piece of paper that when unfolded spells a name.

6. WATCH YOUR STEP

The answer is RICHIE. The two circles are added (16 + 2) to get 18 which refers to the eighteenth letter of the alphabet (R). The squares are added to get 9 which refers to the ninth letter of the alphabet (I). The lone triangle refers to the third letter of the alphabet (C). The pentagon refers to to the eighth letter of the alphabet (H). The cross refers to the ninth letter of the alphabet (I). The star refers to the fifth letter of the alphabet (E).

	2	16					●
●	2						
3	■			6		4	
★			6				2
	8				3	■
5			12	6		
	⬠					
	2				■	3
2		†				9
	4			2	3	▲

7. GUNNING FOR SOMEONE

The matching gun has the initials RW. The differences displayed by the other guns are circled here.

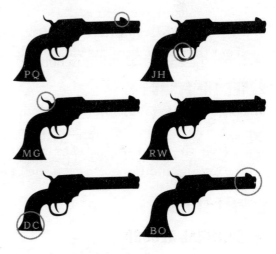

PQ

JH

MG

RW

DC

BO

8. SIGN OF THE TIMES

NAME	TIME ENTERED
Judith Kirton	8:15am
Bob Cross	9:00am
Silvia Taylor	10:30am
Andrew Gatlin	12:35pm
Callum Lozano	1:40pm
Richie Meddit	2:20pm
Amanda Krauss	3:00pm
Robert Wilson	4:10pm
Agnes McDonald	4:30pm

9. TALKING IN CIRCLES

There are ten rounds of interviews in total meaning that the process lasts 90 minutes. Therefore the latest possible time to start conducting interviews is 15:30.

1. IN THE DRIVING SEAT

The correct route is shown above: letters along the path of the solution spell out the postcode of the village hall: RW27 JAV.

2. SEE THE SIGNS

The peculiar thing Emily noticed is that the numbers on the signposts are not distances but instead instructing you to take the letter at that position in the word: for instance the third letter of 'duck pond' is 'C', and so on. The additional location spelt out is: CASTLE.

3. HALL OF FAME

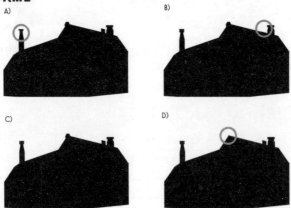

The answer is C. The changes to the other silhouettes of the village hall are shown above.

4. DUTY CALLS

The numerical code, when used in conjunction with the letters displayed on the corresponding numbers on the keypad, spells out the name DEIRDRE. The hyphen character is used to separate letters of the name.

5. THE KEY TO SUCCESS

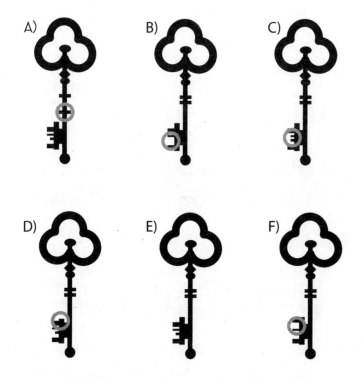

The matching key is E. The differences displayed by the other keys are circled above.

6. CODE NAMES

The code has been created by shifting each letter down the alphabet one position (so the letter 'B' in a name is represented by the letter 'A' in the code, and so on). The names are revealed when the code is reversed: THOMAS GARCIA, SILVIA TAYLOR, GERALD MILLER, ROBERT WILSON, JUDITH KIRTON, OLIVIA HARRIS, ANDREW GATLIN, MARTHA DAVIES, CALLUM LOZANO, RICHIE MEDDIT.

7. STRANGE SIGNS

The symbols used to compose the signature are signs of the zodiac, and respectively represent: Virgo, Aquarius, Leo, Gemini, Libra, Aries, Sagittarius and Scorpio. The first letters of these symbols reveal the identity of the letter writer: VAL GLASS.

8. ILLUMINATION

The residents of each house are:

    1: Wilson family
    3: Richardson family
    5: Smith family
    7: Rashid family
    9: Patel family
  11: Rogers family

Therefore Michael's prime suspects are the Wilson family.

9. ONE TRACK MIND

> I am appalled by the plan to extend the railway line. Have you no regard for the land that this new track will destroy or the wildlife that lives in harmony with us here in Little Riddlewood? I will not simply stand by and let this happen. You have been warned!

To crack the code, turn each number to a letter of the alphabet using A=1, B=2 and so on. It appears that the intended route will be detrimental to the surrounding wildlife of Little Riddlewood, so whoever wrote this letter might have an affinity with nature and the wonderful flora and fauna of the idyllic village.

10. A GAME OF CHESS

A must be the bishop or knight since the square above it would be attacked by the other three pieces. B cannot be the knight. The only pieces that can attack the 3 square with this board setup are the bishop, rook and queen, therefore A, C, E must be these in some order. Since A was a bishop or knight, it must be the bishop. Since B cannot be a knight, bishop, rook or queen this it must be the king, and piece D must be the knight. As E is attacking the 3 square diagonally it must be the queen, and C must be the rook.

Therefore the solution is:

A = bishop, B = king, C = rook, D = knight, E = queen.

11. VEGETABLE MATTER

ANDREW GATLIN   CHARLES PARKER   MARY WILLIAMS   JOHN GILLESPIE

CALLUM LOZANO   RACHEL VAUGHAN   ANNE ROSS

MARIA LINCOLN   JANE FITZGERALD

The answer is ANNE ROSS. The matching turnip is shown above, together with the differences displayed by each of the other turnips.

12. NAME THE DATE

With regard to the month, the first clue rules out February, April, June, July, September, November and December as they are all followed by months of 31 days. The second clue removes January, March, May and October: this just leaves August as the month of the meeting.

With regard to the day of the month, when all the odd numbered and single-digit dates are removed, the remaining options are 10, 12, 14, 16, 18, 20, 22, 24, 26, 28, 30. Of these only the 22nd has digits that sum to four. Therefore the date of the meeting was August 22nd.

13. MINUTE BY MINUTE

The first letters of each line of the excerpt from the minutes spell out the name of one of the suspects: SILVIA TAYLOR.

14. ONLY TIME WILL TELL

The only time that does not appear in the grid, and therefore the time at which Michael and Judith parted company, is 21:05.

Double checking with Deirdre first, Ben assures the team that Judith Kirton did in fact meet Michael at the time he specified.

8	4	8	4	9	2	0	1	0	4
1	1	9	1	1	2	1	8	5	6
3	5	1	2	5	1	8	8	3	1
1	3	1	1	8	3	1	1	9	2
4	3	9	5	7	0	4	9	0	5
9	2	5	0	0	2	4	1	7	3
6	7	1	2	4	4	5	0	4	7
3	1	0	2	7	2	6	9	5	7
8	1	7	3	2	7	8	1	7	4
2	0	4	5	8	2	2	3	1	4

15. SUSPECT PUZZLE

Name	Age	Job	Hobby
Andrew	45	Farmer	Hiking
Callum	28	Teacher	Beekeeping
Richie	33	Doctor	Horticulture
Robert	62	Handyman	Flower Arranging
Silvia	59	Author	Art

1. COPS AND ROBBERS

2. BODY LANGUAGE

The answer is HEART.

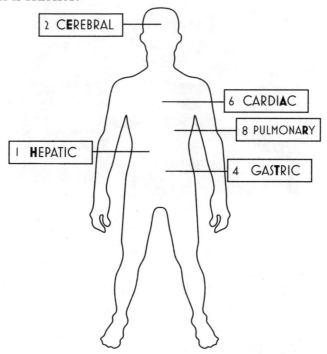

3. CAUSE OF DEATH

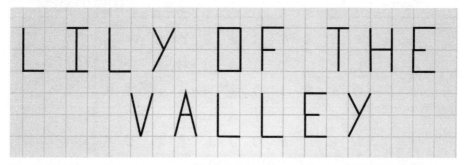

By combining the two lines of partial text together, LILY OF THE VALLEY is revealed.

4. PICTURE THIS

The image depicts a wine glass and bottle – the murderer must have laced the mayor's wine with poison.

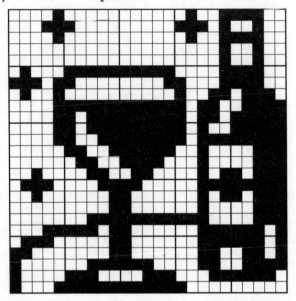

5. A HIDDEN MESSAGE

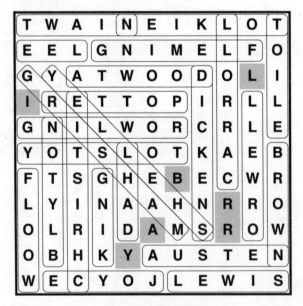

As indicated in the grid above, the unused letters spell out the name of Emily's favourite building, the LIBRARY.

6. BOOKWORM

7. NAME TAG

The images depict a toe and a knee,
so the answer is Tony ('toe knee').

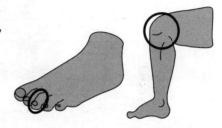

8. BALANCING THE BOOKS

The word that changes is PRINCIPLE/PRINCIPAL. The reissued book
is therefore the one that contains the correct spelling in the context of
the page, which is 'principal'.

9. WRONG NUMBER

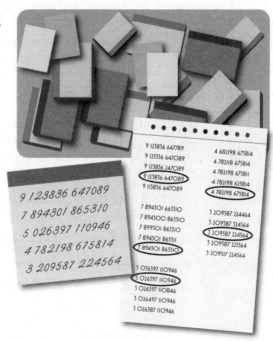

10. CROSS SECTION

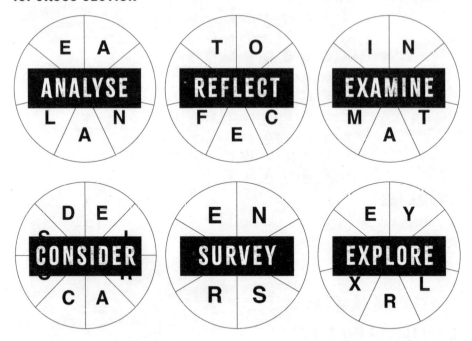

The answers are: analyse, reflect, examine, consider, survey, explore.
The unused letters spell out the section: BOTANY.

11. TALL TALES

The title hints at what to do to solve the puzzle. You must rearrange
the books in height order. This then gives the message:
THE TALLEST BOOK ON THIS SHELF IS THE BOOK
THAT YOU NEED.

12. A CRACKING CODE

The puzzle is a cryptogram in which each letter of the alphabet is
represented by a random different letter, or possibly even itself.
In this code, for instance, the letter 'E' is represented by 'N' in the
code whenever it occurs. Cracking the code reveals the following
information: *When growing lily of the valley plants it is important to
ensure they are positioned in a shady spot and that the surrounding soil
is kept moist.*

13. SHOPPING LIST

Monday
3 x Apple
4 x Onion
5 x Cheese
3 x Butter

Tuesday
2 x Soup
1 x Fish
1 x Flour
3 x Spinach
4 x Chicken
2 x Cereal

As illustrated, what appears to be a shopping list is actually a code that instructs the solver to take the letters at the relevant positions on each line to spell out the instruction: POST OFFICE.

14. EVERY NAME IN THE BOOK

The list of names is in Braille. The names mentioned are as follows:

- Silvia Taylor
- Amelia Miller
- Andrew Gatlin
- Callum Lozano
- Evelyn Pagani
- Joseph Nguyen
- Richie Meddit
- Oliver Bailey

All those who are still suspects have borrowed the book, apart from Robert Wilson.

15. IN BLACK AND WHITE

The number of shaded boxes can be turned to letters of the alphabet to break the code. For instance, one black box = A, two black boxes = B, and so on. The name of the branch manager is revealed to be AUDREY.

1. DOOR TO DOOR

Each number is the previous door number doubled, then three is added. Alternatively you might notice that the differences between the numbers double: 4, 8, 16, 32, 64 and 128.

2. STAMP OF APPROVAL

The train's chimney on the bottom-left stamp is taller than on the others. Therefore, this stamp is the fake.

3. MISSING CONNECTIONS

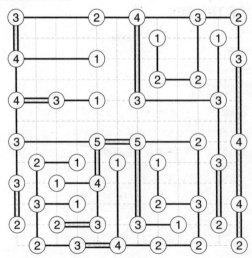

4. HANDLE IT

The sequence shown consists of
11, seven and five-sided shapes.
Since the sequence consists of
prime numbers going backwards,
the crank with the three-sided
shape should be selected next.

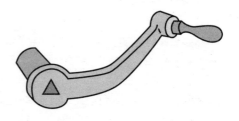

5. KEPT IN THE LOOP

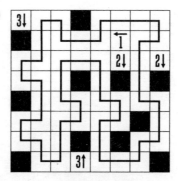

6. SWAPPING NOTES

7. THINK OUTSIDE THE BOX

Path 1:
Collection No: 02378

Room 3

Path 2:
Collection No: 93761

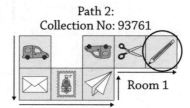

Room 1

Path 3:
Collection No: 04325

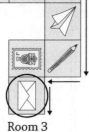

Room 1

Path 4:
Collection No: 85309

Room 1

8. MISSING LINK

Foot <u>R</u> <u>E</u> <u>S</u> <u>T</u> Mass

Life <u>L</u> <u>O</u> <u>N</u> <u>G</u> Distance

Down <u>R</u> <u>I</u> <u>V</u> <u>E</u> <u>R</u> Boat

Ginger <u>B</u> <u>R</u> <u>E</u> <u>A</u> <u>D</u> Winner

Finish <u>L</u> <u>I</u> <u>N</u> <u>E</u> Judge

Prim <u>R</u> <u>O</u> <u>S</u> <u>E</u> Water

Door <u>S</u> <u>T</u> <u>E</u> <u>P</u> Brother

Centre <u>S</u> <u>T</u> <u>A</u> <u>G</u> <u>E</u> Coach

The highlighted letters spell out the word: ENVELOPE.

9. CIRCULAR LOGIC

10. MIXED MESSAGE

Each letter of the alphabet has been swapped with another at random. You must work out the identities of these swaps to crack the code.

Congratulations on your successful application to the Noble Horticultural Guild. As you know membership of this elite society is very exclusive but we were really impressed with the knowledge displayed in your application.

Please find enclosed your welcome pack, Silvia

11. ITEM NUMBER

The answer is TROPICAL FOLIAGE CL. In order to read this, you must fold the rows of numbers on the dotted lines until the words and initials can be read.

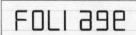

12. SHRED OF EVIDENCE

R	I	C	H	I	E	'	S
O	R	D	E	R		O	F
2		G	A	R	D	E	N
K	N	E	E	L	I	N	G
P	A	D	S		F	O	R
T	A	L	E	N	T	E	D
G	R	O	W	E	R	S	!

13. BEHIND BARS

The barcode is disguising text in Morse code. The thinner bars represent dots and the thicker bars represent dashes. When translated, the text reads:

GARDENING FOR BEGINNERS

Did you find the key at the back of the book?

14. GOING PLACES

The hidden location can be extracted by selecting the letter within the name of each landmark denoted by the numbered bullet point, then ordering these letters to create a word. For example, you must extract the 5th letter in the word 'library' to obtain the letter 'A' and so on.

5. Library   A
3. Police Station   L
11. Village Hall   L
2. Hospital   O
4. Post Office   T
1. Museum   M
10. Supermarket   E
9. Restaurant   N
6. Movie Theatre   T

1. MAKING AN ENTRANCE

If you interpret the clues correctly, the wording below is revealed.

PUBLIC FOOTPATH AHEAD DOGS PROHIBITED
ALLOTMENT ENTRANCE

The bottom sign is translated to ALLOTMENT ENTRANCE. As the sign is pointing to the right, the gang must head right to find the entrance to the allotment. The signs implement the alphabet of the pigpen cipher. Did you manage to find the key at the back of the book?

2. MISSING PERSON

60029 is the only number not found in the grid and therefore the officer who has been assigned that collar number should be contacted and disciplined.

3. A ROSE BY ANY OTHER NAME

ANTI ACORN = Carnation
MORAL DIG = Marigold
MUSHY MERCHANT = Chrysanthemum
RAVEN LED = Lavender
NO GRANDPAS = Snapdragon
HAY GARDEN = Hydrangea

The phrases are anagrams of common flowers. Unfortunately, none of them were used to poison Mayor Malady.

4. OUT OF ORDER

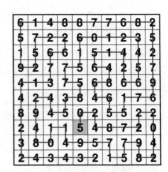

If you interpret the clues correctly the above order is revealed.

5. SPELLING BEE

Once the grid is filled, you must extract the letters in each numbered hexagon in order. When done correctly, the answer word NOTICE is revealed.

6. PEN PUSHER

The key to unlocking this puzzle is the writing implement that has been hung on the noticeboard. This tool has the word 'Ultimate' written on it and when you combine this word with the fact it is written on a pen, you get the word 'penultimate'. This hints at the fact that you must extract the penultimate letters from the notices pinned to the board. The only notice that spells out a coherent combination of letters is the 'Allotment Guidelines' notice. When you scan through each line of text and extract the penultimate letter of each sentence, POTTING SHED is spelled.

7. OPENING NUMBER

The combination to the lock is: 974986957. Now the door can be opened!

9	2	3	8	4	7	6	1	5
1	7	6	2	5	9	3	8	4
5	8	4	6	3	1	2	7	9
2	5	8	9	7	3	4	6	1
6	1	9	5	8	4	7	2	3
3	4	7	1	2	6	5	9	8
7	6	5	3	1	8	9	4	2
4	3	1	7	9	2	8	5	6
8	9	2	4	6	5	1	3	7

8. TABLE SCRAPS

The shelving unit is configured exactly like the periodic table. You must extract the symbols of the relevant elements of the periodic table (found at the back of this book) that correspond to the placement of the items in the pigeonholes. Once they are assembled correctly, the word lubrication is spelled out by the relevant chemical symbols: Lu-Br-I-Ca-Ti-O-N.

9. TALL ORDER

To uncover this answer, you must rearrange the oil cans in height order from smallest to largest. Then read across the letters that are present on the cans to discover the answer word CUPBOARD.

10. PENCIL IN

Once the puzzle is solved, the word TOOLS is revealed. This suggests the team should investigate the tools found within the shed.

11. TOOLS FOR THE JOB

1035. Some of the gardening tools stand for Roman numerals which you must extract in order. The shears look like an X (meaning 10) and so give the first two digits of the code. The garden fork has three prongs which form III (meaning three) which is the third number of the code. Finally, the lopper is closed and looks like a V which stands for five. This is the final digit of the code. The rest of the equipment should be disregarded.

12. PLANT A SEED OF DOUBT

Using the clues outside the grid, you can logically find where each of the lily of the valley plants are found, as shown in the solution grid here:

How peculiar...

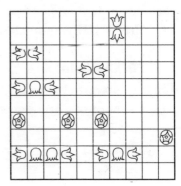

13. MAP OUT

To crack this puzzle, you must overlay the allotment map with the location of the lily of the valley plants revealed by the previous puzzle. Going by this map, only a few members grow lily of the valley and two of them are suspects. If this can be proven, then Callum Lozano can be eliminated as a suspect as he is not growing lily of the valley plants. His bees are sure to be happy!

14. REAP WHAT YOU SOW

The colours on the left and right hold the key to this puzzle. You must match up the colours on the left column to the shade of that colour listed in the right column. Each line intersects one letter in the manufacturer's instructions. Once all the lines are drawn you must rearrange the letters to form a colour. Lily of the valley = Red; Spearmint = Pink; Fuchsia = Blue.

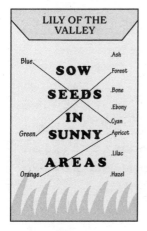
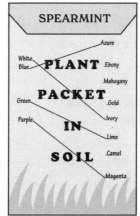
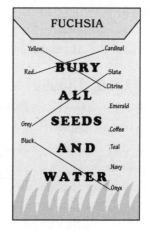

15. BUYING TIME

LONDON. A code word has been hidden in the items on the bookmarked page! The price of each item correlates to a letter in the item name. For example, the fifth letter of 'wheelbarrow' is 'L' and so that letter must be extracted first. The 10th letter of wheelbarrow is 'O' and so this is the next letter to be extracted. You then must move onto the next item and repeat the process.

1. WAVE THE FLAG
The note reads FIND THE CONDUCTOR. The message is written in flag semaphore. Did you find the key at the back of the book?

2. WHISTLE STOP
The notes that must be played, in order, spell out the word DECADE. You can gather this information by looking at the bottom-right notice that appears to be several train tracks but is actually a musical stave in disguise. Conveniently, each whistle is assigned to a conductor and is tuned to the note that begins with the first letter of their name.

3. TRAIN OF THOUGHT
OXFORD, YORK, LONDON, BRISTOL
Each of the trains display their destination in Morse code. You can see that each carriage is one of two types representing a dash or a dot respectively. These can be used to form words corresponding to the destinations of the trains.

4. ALL ON SCHEDULE?
In order to decode the logbook you must reverse the alphabet. For example, A=Z, B=Y C=X and so on and so forth. Once all the letters have been converted, the following message is revealed:

— LOGBOOK —			
ENGINE	DRIVER	STATUS	COMMENTS
SWIFT	MAURICE	CANCELLED	ALL PASSENGERS REIMBURSED
RAPID	HARRY	DELAYED	ENGINEERS CALLED
BRISK	VICTOR	FAULTY	BOOKED FOR SERVICE
TURBO	FREYA	ARRIVED	ALL PASSENGERS PRESENT

It appears that only one train that was due to make the early morning journey to London reached its destination. Now you have to work out if any of the murder suspects were even on the train to begin with!

5. WAITING GAME

The answer is E. Now the team can access the waiting room.

6. ALL ABOARD

The tickets that belongs to Richie Meddit and Silvia Taylor are B and C. In order to figure this out, you need to imagine folding the edges of each ticket so that they are facing each other. In the negative space the initials RM and ST can be seen!

7. MAKING TRACKS

The Memorial Gardens would be destroyed if the plans to extend the train line were to go ahead. What, or who, do the Memorial Gardens commemorate?

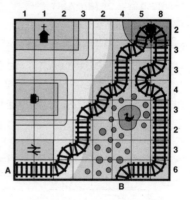

8. GET THE MESSAGE

The answer is GAMBLE WITH DEATH. In order to find this hidden message, you must extract each capital letter from the ransom note in order. This appears to be a very clear death threat. It seems the team are on the trail of the killer!

9. BAD NEWS

In order to discover the answer, you must layer the contents of the advertisement that appears in both newspapers together.

10. SIGN ON THE DOTTED LINE

The names in the petition read RONALD MURPHY, SIENNA TURNER, JULIA KERRY, ROBERT WILSON, CLAUDIA LAWSON, RANDALL MORRIS, SILVIA TAYLOR. You can determine this by by shifting the alphabet two letters, so C in the code represents the letter A, and so on. One name in this list is particularly interesting...

11. BRICK BY BRICK

MARION MEDDIT is the name concealed in the base of the statue. In order to discover this answer, you must analyse the brickwork on the base. Tally marks have been used to log a series of numbers. When you convert these to letters using A=1 and so on, Marion's name is revealed.

12. SPELL IT OUT

The pamphlet has an additional message hidden within the margins of the page. You must assign each line of the pamphlet a letter commencing with A then continue in the order of the alphabet until the final line. The number next to each letter in the margin indicates which letter within each line to extract. For instance, D1 means you should extract the first letter from the fourth line down (line D) to get the letter G which is the first letter of the message. Continue in this manner to reveal the message GRANNY WILL BE REMEMBERED.

13. PROTECT THE PERIMETER

This is the most efficient configuration to organise Inspector Pointer's officers. If Richie tries to escape by train he will surely be apprehended.

1. FOOT IN THE DOOR

Richie Meddit's house number is 37. The rest of the houses along his side of the road appear to display every second prime number from seven upwards.

2. FOOD FOR THOUGHT

All the letters of the alphabet are present on the fridge door besides A, H, I, R, S and Z. These letters, when arranged correctly, spell the word SHIRAZ.

3. OUT OF DATE

28th February - 118 days = 2nd November.

4. STEP IN THE RIGHT DIRECTION

Standing at the shed, the duo need to take seven paces west to reach the spot where Richie buried something.

5. THOUGHT EXPERIMENT

Each of the numbers on the test tubes refer to the atomic number of chemical elements found on the periodic table. When you note down each chemical symbol on the test tubes from left to right, the word POISON can be read. Richie's knowledge of the human body and horticulture make him the perfect person in the village to formulate such a deadly substance!

Phosphorus 15 (P)
Oxygen 8 (O)
Iodine 53 (I)
Sulphur 16 (S)
Oxygen 8 (O)
Nitrogen 7 (N)

6. WRITER'S BLOCK

The keys that have been swapped are A↔O and E↔I. Richie presumably switched these vowel keys on his typewriter keyboard so that anyone looking briefly at his messages would assume they were just nonsense and pay no attention to them. Richie had clearly planned his escape down to the last detail:

1. Install panic room and buy supplies for it
2. Destroy evidence throughout Little Riddlewood
3. Ensure the silence of witnesses to criminal activity
4. Encode notes around house
5. Bury tools and other related materials
6. Set locks to panic room
7. Book plane tickets under alias
8. Lock self in hidden panic room until investigation runs cold

7. POINT THE FINGER

The matching fingerprint is D. The differences displayed by the other fingerprints are circled here.

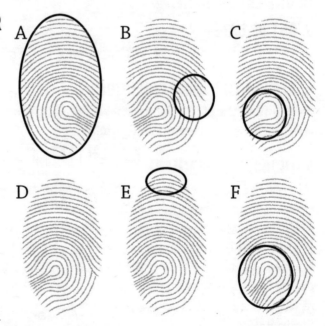

8. ALL THERE IN BLACK AND WHITE

The barcode is actually two words written in highly elongated form, and to read them accurately you must place one of your eyes (with the other closed) at the bottom of the page. From that position, the words PANIC ROOM should be legible.

9. NOTE TO SELF

The message reads:

MUST DELETE BOOK RECORD. TONY WILL HAVE BEHIND DESK.

Richie's code works by swapping adjacent pairs of letters, including spaces (indicated by underscores) and punctuation. This is surprisingly tricky to solve!

10. ZERO IN

BRING POISONED BOTTLE OF SHIRAZ TO MEETING WITH MAYOR AND FEIGN ILLNESS AS AN EXCUSE NOT TO DRINK

This explains Richie's method of escaping the same fate as Mayor Malady! The code has been created using binary, with A denoted as '00001' (1) through to Z denoted as '11010' (26).

11. ONE LAST WORD

S	H	O	W	Y
M	E	A	L	S
G	R	I	P	S
T	O	N	G	S
B	O	G	U	S

12. CUFF 'EM!

The code is solved by summing up the individual digits in each number then converting to a letter. For instance, 576 should be treated as 5+7+6 = 18 = R, and so on.

How could you have known Richie Meddit was the culprit all along? Visit littleriddlewood.com/momm to check your answer.

Richie Meddit you are under arrest for the murder of Mayor Malady. You have the right to remain silent.

SEMAPHORE KEY

BRAILLE KEY

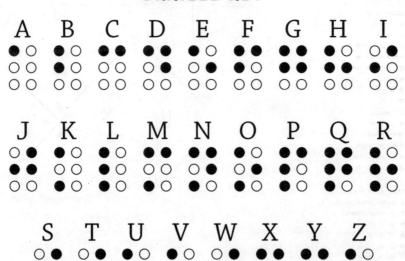

PERIODIC TABLE

1 H																	2 He
3 Li	4 Be											5 B	6 C	7 N	8 O	9 F	10 Ne
11 Na	12 Mg											13 Al	14 Si	15 P	16 S	17 Cl	18 Ar
19 K	20 Ca	21 Sc	22 Ti	23 V	24 Cr	25 Mn	26 Fe	27 Co	28 Ni	29 Cu	30 Zn	31 Ga	32 Ge	33 As	34 Se	35 Br	36 Kr
37 Rb	38 Sr	39 Y	40 Zr	41 Nb	42 Mo	43 Tc	44 Ru	45 Rh	46 Pd	47 Ag	48 Cd	49 In	50 Sn	51 Sb	52 Te	53 I	54 Xe
55 Cs	56 Ba	57 La	72 Hf	73 Ta	74 W	75 Re	76 Os	77 Ir	78 Pt	79 Au	80 Hg	81 Tl	82 Pb	83 Bi	84 Po	85 At	86 Rn
87 Fr	88 Ra	89 Ac	104 Rf	105 Db	106 Sg	107 Bh	108 Hs	109 Mt	110 Ds	111 Rg	112 Cn	113 Nh	114 Fl	115 Mc	116 Lv	117 Ts	118 Og

58 Ce	59 Pr	60 Nd	61 Pm	62 Sm	63 Eu	64 Gd	65 Tb	66 Dy	67 Ho	68 Er	69 Tm	70 Yb	71 Lu
90 Th	91 Pa	92 U	93 Np	94 Pu	95 Am	96 Cm	97 Bk	98 Cf	99 Es	100 Fm	101 Md	102 No	103 Lr

MORSE CODE

PIGPEN CIPHER

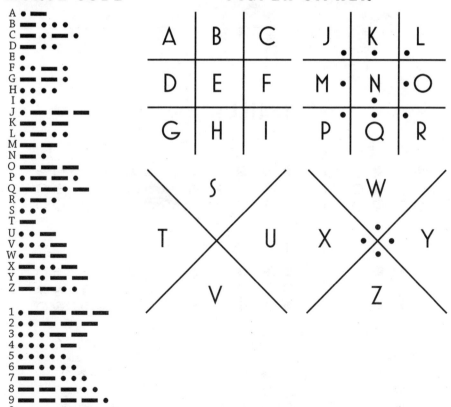

ACKNOWLEDGEMENTS

I would like to thank Rebecca Uffindell, Andy Harwood and Amy Smith for their invaluable assistance with the creation of the storyline, artwork and layout of this book.

Dan Moore
🐦@danm00re